I watch, and am as a sparrow alone upon the house top.
Psalm 102:7 KJV

Sparrow on a Housetop

WWII Aftermath

Billie Houston

Published by Chavelbooks LLC, 2022.

SPARROW ON A HOUSETOP

First edition. March 3, 2022.

Copyright © 2022 Billie Houston.

ISBN: 979-8201036683

Written by Billie Houston.

Table of Contents

Chapter One

Sara Holden pulled her team of mules to a halt and wiped her brow with her shirt sleeve. Two o'clock in the afternoon on a hot Texas day was not an ideal time to be compacting soil over newly planted cotton seed. She pushed back her split bonnet. Her dark hair clung to her head in curls wet with perspiration.

"Sara! Sara!" Her mother ran from the back door of the farmhouse and raced down a worn path toward the cotton patch.

Instantly realizing something must be wrong, Sara dropped her reins and ran toward her mother. A half dozen disturbing questions raced through her brain. Had Daddy taken a turn for the worse? Did Grandma have another heart attack? Bad news about James or Kent? *No, not Kent.*

Dora Carson skidded to a halt, narrowly avoiding colliding with her daughter. "The Germans surrendered unconditionally." Her breath came in gasps. "The war in Europe is over." *Pant* "Praise the Lord." *Puff* "James and Kent will be coming home soon."

"Mama, slow down before you are the one having the heart attack."

"Phooey," Dora scoffed. "I'm as strong as a Missouri mule."

"And about as stubborn." Dora *was* a little woman in stature and structure, but she had a relentless determination, and a will of iron. "A puff of wind could blow you over. How did you find out about the war in Europe being over?"

"Moses Gentry told me. He had to go to town to get a new part for his tractor. He stopped by on his way home. Everybody in Cedar Gap is talking about the Germans finally yelling calf rope."

"What about the Japanese? Did the postman come? Did I get a letter from Kent?"

"No, the Japanese didn't surrender. Yes, the postman came. No, you didn't get a letter. Your husband is coming home. He can't waste his time writing. Get on with your compacting. I gotta go back to Daddy and Grandma."

Sara watched her mother walk back up the path toward the old farmhouse. Both Kent and James were coming home. Thank God. She and Mama couldn't have held on much longer. Having her brother and her husband here meant they could run the farm and she could help Mama with Daddy and Grandma. She drank from her canteen, and went back to work compacting the seeds she and Mama planted yesterday. Her heart sang with joy. Kent was coming home. She hadn't seen him in almost two years. Had he changed? Of course, he had. A man couldn't wage bloody warfare in Africa, through Italy, across France and into Germany, and not change.

God, thank you for keeping him alive all that time. Please, let him come home soon.

****

Later that evening, Sara marked her place and put her book on the table beside her. It had been a long day. She was bone-weary, but she doubted she could sleep. Too many uncertainties danced through her head.

Mama laid her Bible aside, stretched and yawned. "We should start planning a homecoming meal for our soldier boys. I'll have to count our ration stamps. If Kent likes chicken and dumplings, I'll kill that old Ancona rooster. I can cook him in the pressure cooker, and make him tender and juicy." She leaned back in her rocker. Light from the kerosene lamp cast shadows across her face and high-lighted the silver in her hair. "I can make a fresh peach cobbler. Does Kent like peaches?"

One fact swept through Sara's mind, blowing away every other nagging doubt. She didn't know what her husband liked to eat. She didn't know anything about him, except that she loved him. "Should I sleep in Grandma's room tonight?"

"It would be best if you did. She takes medicine at two-thirty. I set her alarm clock for two-fifteen." Mama stood and walked toward the front door. "Gotta make sure everything is locked and secure. I don't want Daddy waking up, going outside, and wandering away somewhere. I'll be glad when he starts getting bet-ter."

Daddy wasn't going to get better. He was only going to get worse. Sara knew that, and she suspected her mother did too. "Mama, sit back down for a minute. We have to talk about Daddy."

Dora stopped. "I don't know what there is to say." She retraced her footsteps and sat in her rocker. "You've been itching to have this conversation for a long time. Go ahead, speak up."

"We have to face facts about Daddy."

"I married your daddy when I was sixteen years old. He was eighteen. Everybody said it wouldn't last. Everybody was wrong. It lasted. We lasted. I love him. He loves me. He's always been my rock and my fortress. Those are the facts."

"Daddy's not well." Sara spoke words that broke her heart. "His body may still be sound, but his mind is slipping. If there is a way to help him, we have to find it."

"Daddy is not your problem. It's up to me, with God's help, to take care of him. Now, about tomorrow. Moses will be by early. He will haul our produce to town. You can go along with him. I made a grocery list. Praise the Lord James is coming home. He can fix the car. It will be nice to have our own transportation again—"

"Mama, stop changing the subject. You can't ignore Daddy's condition any longer." Always before when her mother refused to talk about Daddy, Sara backed away. Not this time. "We have to face this and find a way to cope."

"Sara, darling,'" Dora spoke softly. "Have I ever butted into your marriage?" She answered her own question. "No, I haven't, though heaven knows I've wanted to plenty of times."

"This is different. Mama, please—"

"It's different to you maybe, but not to me." Dora stood. "I'm sending six dozen eggs, too. Watch that produce manager at the grocery store. He will cheat you if you give him half a chance."

"Mama, please—"

"Good night, daughter." Without bothering to look back, Dora walked toward the front door.

Chapter Two

May 11, 1945
Friday Morning

Sara climbed into the passenger side of Moses Gentry's old International Harvester pickup, and slammed the door.

Moses stepped on the starter. The pickup coughed to life, and took off with a lurch.

Sara had known Moses all her life. He was in the same high school graduating class as her older brother James. He was a widower with two small children, a boy and a girl. She appreciated his help over the last year. "Mama and I are grateful to you for all you have done for us since Daddy has been sick."

"I'm glad I could help." Moses slowed as a rabbit raced across the road in front of him. "It's my contribution to the war effort since I can't go and fight."

"Why not?" Moses' deep frown told her she had touched a nerve. "I'm sorry. It's none of my business."

He glanced briefly in her direction. "It's no secret. I was two months too old for the draft in nineteen-forty." He turned his gaze back to the road. "By the time they raised the draft age, Mary had passed away and I was the sole support of two young children. When Uncle Sam moved the draft age from twenty-seven to thirty-seven, I was deferred because of the kids, and because the government thought it was more important for me to supply food and cotton to the army than it was to fight for my country." He paused before adding, "There was another consideration, too. I am a licensed and ordained Baptist minister."

"Preachers aren't drafted?"

"Neither ministers of religion, nor divinity students."

"I see."

"Do you?" A touch of irony sounded in his voice. He stopped before turning onto the road that led to Cedar Gap. Out of the blue, he asked, "When will your husband be coming home?"

"I don't know yet."

"Isn't his name Kent?"

"Yes, why do you ask?"

"I never knew a man with Kent for a given name."

"It's Kent." The name tasted sweet on her tongue. "His name is Kent Holden."

"Will you be moving back to Orange when he returns?"

"We haven't made any plans."

They were coming to the outskirts of Cedar Gap.

"Do you like his family?" Moses turned toward Main Street.

Sara's mind was miles away. Where was Kent now? How long before she could hold him in her arms again? Belatedly Moses' question registered. "What?"

"Your in-laws, do you like them?" He drove around the grocery store and backed to the loading dock.

"I don't know them that well." Truthfully, she didn't know them at all. She was not even sure they knew she existed. She got out of the pickup before he could ask more questions.

Mama was right about the produce manager. He bore watching. More than once, she called his hand as he tried to cheat her. They were arguing when Moses stepped in. "Stop trying to cheat Sara, Joe. If her money doesn't tally with the produce she brought in, Dora Carson will come in here tomorrow and be all over you like stink on a skunk."

"Did I make a mistake?" Joe wiped his hands on his dirty apron. "Sorry, Preacher. Let's start over."

After that, things went more smoothly. Sara sold her produce and collected her money. As she and Moses went from the back into the front of the grocery store, she asked, "Why wasn't Joe drafted? He looks hale and hearty to me."

"He was born with a club foot." Moses gave Sara his grocery list, his ration books, and two ten-dollar bills. "I have business at the bank. If you can get these things for me, I'll be back to pick you up in about an hour."

"I'll save your change." Sara took the proffered items. She enjoyed shopping. Soon she would be shopping for her and Kent. They could build a little house on the ridge in the south pasture. James could help. He was a good carpenter. So was Moses. Maybe he could be persuaded to lend a hand. *Oh, Kent, we are going to be so happy.*

*****

Moses was pulling onto the road that led out of Cedar Gap when he said, "You got a V-Mail from your husband." He took the small envelope from his shirt pocket. "He's a staff sergeant in the Thirty-Sixth Division. I'm impressed."
Sara grabbed the letter and tore it open. Her eyes filled with tears as she silently read:

April 29, 1945
Somewhere in France

Hello Darling,
Very little time. We are moving out again. Rumor is the Germans are ready to sur-
render. If it's true, I will be home soon. I love you. Kent
"Bad news?" Moses put his arm out the window to signal a right turn.
"No. It's good news."
"Then why are you crying?"
"These are tears of happiness." She slipped the letter into her purse. "Kent suspected when he wrote this letter on April 29th." She patted her handbag. "That the Germans were about to surrender." Moses' remark about being impressed by Kent's rank filtered through her thoughts. "Why should you be impressed by Kent being a staff sergeant? There must be hundreds, maybe thousands of staff sergeants in the army."
"It's not that." Moses turned onto the unpaved road that led to the Carson farm. "He's in the 36th Division. I've been reading in the newspapers about their bravery. Those men are all heroes."
"I hope he doesn't end up a dead hero." Sara stared out the window at the passing scenery. The countryside was ablaze with wild flowers – bluebonnets, Texas pinks, sweet Williams, buttercups, and Indian blankets covered the pastures, ditches, and roadside in a riot of colors. "How can there be so much beauty in a world so filled with injustice and hate?"
"I could answer with one of a half dozen platitudes." Moses slowed his pickup to a snail's pace, as they neared the turn that led to the Carson drive. "They would be empty rhetoric. God leads each person to find his or her own answers." He pulled into the farm's driveway. "I will pray for you."

"Don't bother." Sudden, futile anger exploded inside Sara. "I have been listening to platitudes and uttering prayers all my life. What has it gotten me besides hardships and heartache?"

"I gave you an honest answer. If it offended you, I'm sorry." He stopped his pickup, got out, and moved toward the bed of the truck.

Sara got out, slammed the door, and moved to stand across from him. "I'm sorry, too. I didn't mean what I said. Forgive me."

Moses heisted a bag of groceries into each arm, and walked toward the back door. "Sure. Let's get this stuff inside. I need to get home."

Sara grabbed a bag of groceries and followed along behind him. She had offended the man who had been her lifeline through the last year and a half. "I'm not angry with you. I am mad at life in general. Why should a thief like Joe be here at home when Kent is so far from away, fighting for Joe's right to practice dishonesty? Life is so unfair."

Moses looked back over his shoulder. "You shouldn't question God." He picked up his pace.

Sara trailed along behind. *Maybe I shouldn't, but sometimes I do. I can't help it.*

Chapter Three

May 13, 1945
Sunday Evening

Sara dried the last of the dishes. "That was a good supper, Mama. Nobody in the world makes better cornbread than you do."

"I've had lots of practice." Dora wiped the surface of the oilcloth-covered kitchen table with her cup towel. "When Daddy asked me to marry him, he said, 'Dora, one reason I am proposing to you is you make the best cornbread in Cedar County.'"

"He didn't really say that, did he?" Sara sat on the bench that stood along one side of the table.

"He did." Dora pulled out a chair and sat across from her daughter. "He said a lot of other things, too." She smiled and her blue eyes twinkled. "I'm not telling you what else, so don't ask."

"Daddy didn't eat any cornbread tonight. He didn't eat much of anything." Sara drew a long breath. Kent was coming home, and soon. It's time she told the truth. "Mama, we have to talk."

"Don't start about Daddy again tonight."

"It's not about Daddy. It's about Kent, and me."

"Something tells me this isn't going to be good news." Dora's smile disappeared, and the twinkle vanished from her eyes.

'It's not anything bad, either. I should have told you long ago, but after you said what you did about us getting married after we had known each other for only six months. I decided not to."

"I have no idea what you are talking about." Dora shook her head and shrugged. "You said six months wasn't long enough to know a man before you married him. You said..."

"Things are different for your generation, what with the war and all. Maybe six months is long enough." Dora dropped her hands into her lap and stared into space. "I've known Daddy all my life. When I started to school, he was in the third grade. He used to tease me, and I would chase him around the school-yard."

"That's not all." Why must her mother choose now, of all times, to reminisce about Daddy? Sara drew another deep breath. *I have to tell her, and it has to be now.* "I really only knew Kent three days before I married him. He's been divorced twice, and he's thirty-five years old." She closed her eyes and clenched her teeth.

Dora jumped from her chair. It tumbled backward behind her. "My Lord, child, your husband is might-near as old as your daddy. Two divorces? You only knew him two days? What were you thinking?"

"Three days, Mama, I knew him *three* days." Sara walked around the table, and up righted her mother's chair. "He's nowhere near as old as Daddy. Sit down and I will explain."

Dora sat. "Where was your Aunt Mollie all this time? She was supposed to be taking care of you. If I can't trust my only sister, who can I trust?"

"I was twenty-one years old when I went to Orange to work. I could take care of myself." The last thing Sara wanted to do was cause trouble between Mama and Aunt Mollie. "I am not going to tell you anything else until you promise not to blame Aunt Mollie for my marriage to Kent. It was my decision. I was of age. Aunt Mollie couldn't have stopped me, even if she tried."

"Which, evidently, she didn't."

"She didn't know until after we were married." What a tangled web she had woven. "I moved out of Aunt Mollie's house two weeks after I got to Orange."

Once more, Dora was on her feet. She came to stand eye-to-eye with her daughter. The disappointment in her gaze made Sara drop her head and stare at the floor. "I had to sleep on the couch at Aunt Mollie's house. I got the opportunity to move in with Betty Jean when her old roommate married and moved away. I took it."

"You moved into a house with a woman you had known only two weeks?"

"It was an apartment." Sara moved back to the bench, and sat down.

"You moved, but you let me keep sending you letters to Mollie's address. You had her return address on your letters. The two of you betrayed me." Dora sat in her chair and rested her arms on the table. "How could you lie to me all this time?" Her eyes filled with tears.

Sara's heart ached. She had wounded her mother deeply. "When I got home, Grandma and Daddy were both sick. I came home to help you care for them, not to give you something else to worry about." It seemed such a little thing then. "I didn't lie, exactly. I just neglected to tell all the truth. You assumed because I had been in Orange six months that was how long I had known Kent. I didn't correct you."

"Two divorces? He's thirty-five years old? This will never last." Tears streamed down Dora's cheeks. "You mustn't tell Daddy or Grandma what you just told me."

Sara expected her mother to be upset by her confession. She never thought she would view it as a catastrophe. Why was she making such a big deal of this? "I'm not ashamed of anything I've done, and I'm not going to hide it, or lie about it, any longer."

Daddy's voice called from down the hall. "Dora? Where are you? I can't find you. Dora?"

"Coming, Angus." Dora jumped to her feet. "Go to bed. We can talk in the morning. If you need help with Grandma during the night, call me." She hurried away.

Sara picked up the kerosene lamp, and walked toward Grandma's room. Mama would love Kent when she got to know him. He was the dearest, sweetest person Sara had ever met.

She tiptoed into Grandma's room, put the lamp on a table in the corner and sat down on the steel cot that was her temporary bed.

"Sara?" Grandma sat up in bed. "Is Dora over her temper tantrum?" Belle Anne Lawson Murray was Dora's mother. Their resemblance was remarkable. They were both short in stature and slim as a reed. Their eyes were cobalt blue. Dora's hair was black, thick, and streaked with gray. Belle's hair was thinning and white as the driven snow. *I'm a carbon copy of them. My hair will someday be gray, and my face as old and wrinkled as a road map.*

"The walls are thin in this old farm house. It's hard *not* to hear. Do you want to talk about it?"

Sara hesitated. "It's not important." She did want to talk about it. Maybe talking would help clear her mind. However, she didn't want to burden her grandma with her problems. "Go to sleep, and don't worry."

"What a foolish child you are." Grandma sat on the side of the bed and slipped her feet into her house shoes. "I will worry more not knowing than I will if I know."

That was all the encouragement Sara needed. "It's long and complicated."

"All I have is time." Grandma reached for her robe.

Chapter Four

May 13, 1945
Sunday Night

Belle moved to her rocker and sat down. "It's like old times, you coming in to talk to your grandma. Tell me what's troubling you."

Sara scooted back on the cot, and leaned against the wall. "How much did you hear?"

"I heard enough to know you married your man after you had known him for only three days. I know you lived with some friend and let your mama think you were at Mollie's house. How did this all come about?"

"Mama didn't want me to go to work in the shipyards in the first place. She agreed after Aunt Mollie said I could live with her. Mama wanted to keep me here, under her wing."

"And you," Grandma said, with a nod of her head, "wanted to get away and try *your* wings."

"I felt guilty about leaving, even though I was twenty-one years old."

"If you had been thirty-one Dora wouldn't have wanted you to leave. She saw you as a little girl. I suspect she always will." Belle yawned. "Go on, tell me the rest of your story."

"There's not much else to tell." Sara leaned forward, and began the process of removing her shoes. "I met Kent at the USO Club. My roommate Betty Jean and I went there every Saturday night to serve coffee and donuts to the service men." She slid her shoes from her feet, and pushed them under her cot. "I knew at first glance he wasn't like the other military men who came into the club. He asked for coffee. I served him and gave him a donut too. He asked my name and I told him. He told me he was Kent Holden. It was as if I had known him all my life. Despite that, there was an air of mystery about him that intrigued me. We talked until the club closed." She turned her head and studied her grandmother's passive face. *What is she thinking?* "Does that sound foolish to you?"

"No, not at all. I fell in love with your grandpa the first time I saw him. I was at a barn dance. I knew the moment he came through the doors he was the one for me."

"Did Grandpa Jasper know, too?"

"He knew all right, but being one of the slow-talking, thorough thinking Murray boys, it took him two years to get around to asking me to marry him. Enough about Grandpa and me. Get on with your story."

"Kent came back the next night and asked me to go for a walk with him. I can't believe I said yes, but I did." Sara snapped her fingers. "Just like that, I agreed to go off with a complete stranger. By the time he walked me home, I knew I was in love with him."

"Huh," Grandma grunted. "That must have been some walk. Where did you go? What did you do?"

"We went to a malt shop and ate ice cream sundaes, and then sat there in the booth and talked until it was closing time." Remembering made Sara smile. "The owner finally asked us to leave."

"I couldn't sleep that night. I kept remembering that Kent was going to ship out in a week. I was afraid I was going to lose him, and just when I had found him. He promised he'd pick me up the next day after work. When I was with him, I was so sure he would. After he left, and I was alone, I was beset by all sorts of doubts. What if he didn't come back? What if I never saw him again?"

"Oh, child." A note of pity sounded in Belle's voice. "Being young and in love is a strange mixture of anxiety and happiness." She struggled to her feet. "Being old and remembering love is much the same. It's time I got to bed. Sleep in your room tonight. I can manage alone."

"I'd rather stay in here." Sara slipped from her dress, and lay down on her cot. "I've wanted for such a long time to share my story about Kent with someone."

"I'm glad that someone is me." Grandma took off her robe and crawled into her bed. "Tell me all about Kent. I'm waiting to hear."

"He's very handsome. His eyes are brown, not a cold brown, but warm like hot chocolate, and soft like velvet. His hair is red. Not a fire-engine red, but a beautiful reddish-brown. He's tall, about six feet. His shoulders are broad and his hips are narrow." Sara put her hands beneath her head and stared at the ceiling. "He's the handsomest man I ever saw, and he's kind too, and gentle, and loving."

"Go on," Grandma urged.

"Kent brought flowers when he came to pick me up after work. He wanted to take me to dinner. I couldn't go to a restaurant in my work overalls. He took me home, and waited for me to shower and dress. He met Betty Jean. They talked while I got ready. Betty Jean was impressed. She told me later that he wasn't like the GIs she met. All they wanted was to sleep with you, and then get shipped out to some other place. Grandma, are you listening?"

Grandma grunted, "Uh huh."

"At the restaurant, Kent proposed to me. I was so surprised. I was even more surprised when I said yes. To make a long story short, Kent had to get permission from his commanding officer to get married. I don't know how he managed to do that, but he did. He even got a special license. We were married the next day by a justice of the peace. Don't tell Mama that. She would be even more upset. She thinks a marriage isn't valid unless it's performed by a preacher. Grandma?"

"I'm here."

"My boss was nice enough to give me the rest of the week off. Kent took me to a hotel in Galveston. It was like a resort. We had four glorious days together. I never knew love could be so wonderful. Being near Kent, and having him hold me in his arms was total bliss. It was all over too soon. The next Monday he shipped out, and I went back to work."

"Grandma, there are so many things I want to ask you, intimate things. Grandma?"

This time Sara's answer was one of Grandma's snores. How long had she been talking to herself?

Chapter Five

June 16, 1945
Saturday Morning

Sara climbed into the passenger seat of her daddy's 1936 Chevy pickup. "I am perfectly capable of driving myself to Cedar Gap. I don't need my brother tagging along to help me bring my husband home."

James got into the driver's seat and pumped the accelerator several times. "You haven't changed a bit. You're just as stubborn now as you were when I left for the army three years ago." He pushed his foot down on the starter. "This old jalopy may or may not make it to Cedar Gap. I don't want you stranded along the road somewhere between here and there." The motor hiccupped to a start, and he drove toward the gate.

Maybe Sara hadn't changed, but James had. The James who went away was a happy-go-lucky, fun-loving boy. This James was a quiet, distant man. She didn't know this James. She wondered if she'd ever have her brother back.

James stopped at the gate. "On the way to town I need to talk to you."

"About what?" Sara got out of the pickup and hurried to the gate. She opened it, and he drove through. As she climbed back into the pickup, she asked again, "What do we need to talk about?" Not a breeze stirred. "It's going to be hot today."

"It's always hot this time of year. What time does Kent's bus get to Cedar Gap?" James turned onto the gravel road.

"It's due at one o'clock, but you know how that goes." Perspiration ran down Sara's face and collected under her arms. "Tell me what you wanted to tell me."

"Do you remember Peggy Sue Brown?"

"Do you mean Peggy Sue Yates? I know she married Charlie Yates, and he was killed fighting somewhere in the South Pacific. She had a baby, a little boy. He must be almost three years old by now."

"He's over three," James said with an assurance that was unsettling.

"How do you know that?" Sara turned to stare at her brother.

"Peggy Sue told me his age in a letter she wrote me about a year ago."

Sara didn't like the sound of that. "Why would she be writing to you?"

"Moses was asking church members to write to boys in our congregation who were fighting overseas. Peggy chose me as her pen pal. I answered back. We've been corresponding ever since." He grinned, and for a moment, he looked like the brother who marched off to war three years ago. He sobered suddenly. "Peggy and I got married last week."

Sara was set to tell her brother that he hadn't been home quite two months. How could he marry someone he'd been seeing for such a short time? Then she remembered Kent, and swallowed her comment. "Have you told Mama?"

"I have. She's not very happy about it." James slowed the pickup as they neared the road that led to Cedar Gap. "She says I should have waited until I was sure. What I didn't dare tell her is that we couldn't wait. Peggy Sue thinks she's pregnant." He made a right turn toward Cedar Gap. "Go ahead, tell me what a rotten person I am."

Later Sara might do that. Now all she could think of was Kent. "Can you drive a little faster?" The nearer they got to Cedar Gap, the more excited Sara became. "I have waited for this day for such a long time."

"Have a little patience." James glanced briefly in her direction. "So, what do you think?" He pulled his gaze back to the road.

"I think that for just once, the bus had better be on time." Sara leaned forward. "You will like Kent. He's such a wonderful man."

"I'm sure I will." James waved one hand. "Peggy Sue and her son will be moving in with us next week. I'm bringing her and little Junior to the house for Sunday dinner. All the family will be together for the first time in in such a long time."

Peggy Sue and Junior weren't family to her. Sara pushed that thought aside. She would solve that problem when the time came. At the moment, all she could think about was Kent coming home.

June 16, 1945
Saturday Evening

Kent did justice to Mama's welcome-home supper. He had a second helping of chicken and dumplings and ate a generous serving of peach cobbler. "That was a mighty fine meal, Mrs. Carson."

Mama hadn't thawed completely, but she was softening. "Much obliged, Sergeant. I'm pleased you enjoyed it." Conversation drifted from food to crops before James and Keith began discussing the recent war in Europe. Sara wanted to tell them to shut up. She had been on pins and needles since they returned from Cedar Gap. Now, what she wanted was to take Kent to her bedroom and make love.

"Was I in a war once?" Daddy turned to Mama. "I can't recollect for sure."

Grandma, who had until now been as silent as a tomb, spoke. "You were never in a war, Angus. Where ever did you get such an idea?"

Angus's "I was too" collided with Dora's "Mama, I have told you."

Mama and Grandma glared at each other. This was taking on the trappings of a full-fledged war of words. Sara had worried that her family would not accept Kent. If Mama and Grandma got into a battle royal, he might have reservations about accepting *them*. "It doesn't matter. Mama. Why don't you put Daddy to bed? James and I will do the dishes."

"Good idea," James agreed.

"I don't want to go to bed," Angus protested.

"I'll tell you a story." Dora took his hand, and led him from the room.

Grandma scooted her chair back and stood. "James and I will clean the kitchen. You run along, Sara, and have some alone time with your man."

Sara hesitated. "But Grandma—"

"Go on. Git," Grandma flapped her apron in their direction to shoo the couple from the room.

Sara took Kent's hand and led him down the hall and toward the room she had claimed as her own since she was a little girl. "Grandma gets a little bossy sometimes."

"She barks orders like a top sergeant." Kent held onto Sara's hand. "How long has she lived with your parents?"

"They live with her. The farm belongs to Grandma." Sara opened the door to her bedroom and stepped back. "Welcome home, darling."

Kent scooped her into his arms. "Alone at last." He carried her inside, and nudged the door shut with his foot.

Chapter Six

June 17, 1945
Sunday Morning

Sara woke to see sunlight pouring through an east window. She turned to find Kent beside her, stretched out, and sound asleep. She slipped from the bed and put on her robe with the thought that she would bring him breakfast. She was almost to the door when he asked, "Where are you going?" His voice was warm and deep.

She turned and saw the look of love on his face. Her heart melted. "I was going to bring you breakfast in bed."

"Forget breakfast and come back to bed. We have so many plans to make."

Sara got back into bed and snuggled close to her husband. "What kind of plans?"

"For starters, we need to plan our trip to see Mother and Father. They are anxious to see me and meet you."

"Tell me about your parents." Something akin to fear skipped down Sara's backbone. "What have you told them about me?"

"I've told them how beautiful you are, and how much I love you."

Sara was always uncomfortable when someone called her beautiful because she knew she wasn't. She was too skinny and too short. Freckles dusted across her nose, and her eyes were too large for the rest of her face. *Lord, please let them like me.* "When do you want to go?"

"This afternoon if James can drive us to town." Kent kissed the tip of her nose.

"James is bringing his new wife and her son over for Sunday dinner. He wants all the family to be together. Can we make it Monday morning?" She shivered at his touch.

"Monday morning is fine." Kent slid from the bed and began the process of dressing. "Your brother is married?"

"Yes, since last week." Why did she feel so uncomfortable saying that?

"What's the lucky girl's name?"

"Peggy Sue Yates, and she's no girl. Her first husband was killed in the South Pacific. She has a three-year-old son."

"Where's the bathroom?" Kent laced and tied his boots and stood.

Could it be that her husband hadn't been to the privy since he'd arrived? That was impossible. "We have an outhouse. For heaven's sake where have you been going when you needed to relieve yourself?" Heat fused her cheeks and burned her neck.

"I asked James where to go. He said 'behind any tree.'"

She just might kill her brother. If she did, it would be justifiable homicide. "It's that little house beside the barn. Would you like me to go with you?"

"I can find my way." His voice held a note of laughter. He went through the door and closed it behind him.

Sara couldn't remember ever being more embarrassed. She had assumed Kent would know where the bathroom was. James only made it worse. Behind any tree! How could he?

When Kent returned, he was still smiling. "I washed my hands at the kitchen sink. I hope that's okay."

"It's fine." Sara sat on the side of the just-made bed. She wore her Sunday dress and had her Bible and her purse beside her. "Let's have breakfast." She took his arm. "The women at church are going to be green with envy when they see my handsome husband."

They were midway down the hall before he stopped. "We are going to church?"

"Did you forget it's Sunday?" She squeezed his arm.

"I must have." It wasn't his words, but his disturbed tone that bothered her. She opened her mouth to question, and then changed her mind. She shouldn't find fault with his tone of voice.

"I can't go to church with you." Kent turned to look at her. "I have some things to attend to."

"This is Sunday." She had so looked forward to taking him to church.

"I have to fill out some important army papers, and get them in the mail as soon as possible. I'm sorry."

"You can do that—" Sara began, and stopped abruptly. The finality of his answer made her decide to let it go.

June 17, 1945
Sunday Noon

The dining room table groaned beneath the load of Mama's sumptuous noon meal.

"Everything looks so good, Miz Carson." Peggy Sue stood her son on the floor. "Is there something I can do to help?"

Sara was shocked by the changes in Peggy Sue's appearance. She was twenty pounds heavier than when she sat behind Sara in math class in high school. Her hair was short, bleached, and frizzed with a permanent wave.

"Everything's ready," Mama answered. "You just sit down," she pointed. "Right over there. James, you sit by her."

"Yes, ma'am." Peggy Sue scooped Junior up into her arms and followed Mama's directions.

Mama arranged everyone around the table. Grandma, Sara, and Kent sat on one side. James, Peggy Sue, and Junior sat on the other. She put Daddy at the head of the table, next to Sara, and took her place at the other end. "Sara, you can help Daddy put food on his plate."

"I don't need no help." Angus turned to Sara and repeated, "I don't need no help."

"Of course, you don't, Daddy." Sara put her hand over her father's wrist. "Say grace so we can have our meal."

Angus bowed his head, and prayed a rambling prayer, but neglected to ask God's blessing on the food. Just when Sara was set to interrupt, he pronounced a heartfelt, "Amen."

"Miz Carson, I appreciate you putting pillows in Junior's chair so's he can reach the table." Peggy Sue smiled at James. "Your mama is so thoughtful."

"I had youngens of my own once," Mama said, before addressing Sara. "Help your daddy with his napkin."

Sara obeyed.

Peggy Sue tucked Junior's napkin under his chin. He promptly pulled it away and threw it in the floor. She could almost feel sorry for Peggy Sue. The poor woman was trying so hard to make a good impression. She was trying too hard.

Junior let out a yell that could be heard in the next county. "Me want that!" He pointed to Mama's three-layer maple-pecan cake that sat on the dining room buffet.

"You have to eat your chicken and potatoes first." Peggy Sue picked up Junior's discarded napkin and once more tucked it in the neck of his shirt. "Look, yum, yum." She took a bite of her chicken breast.

James cleared his throat before saying, "Moses preached a good sermon this morning."

"He did that," Grandma agreed.

"I thought so, too." Sara was set to say more when Junior let go with another war whoop as he threw his spoon across the table. It missed Grandma's head by a fraction of an inch.

"I'm so sorry, Miz Murray." Peggy Sue jumped to her feet and burst into tears.

"It's all right, sweetheart." James stood and took her in his arms. "Boys get out-of-hand sometimes." He looked over Peggy Sue's shoulder, and directly into Junior's eyes. "Stop that, young man, right now, if want to get a piece of cake after you eat your chicken and potatoes."

Sara stole a glance in Kent's direction. He pressed his napkin to his lips. The amusement in his eyes told her that he was doing his best to suppress a laugh. He was laughing at her family. What must he be thinking?

Junior picked up his chicken leg, and bit into it.

James gave him a spoon. "If you throw this one, you will not have any cake."

A subdued Junior shoved a spoonful of potatoes into his mouth, and chewed as he watched James' every move.

Peggy Sue was still apologizing as James helped her to her chair. "I am so sorry. He don't usually behave this way. I don't know what got into him."

"I can tell you." Grandma pointed her fork in Junior's direction. "He needs a firm hand. Seems like James can handle him. Sit down and finish your dinner and relax. Nobody here is going to bite you."

The remainder of the meal went smoothly. Peggy Sue relaxed. Daddy nodded off to sleep. Mama didn't make a single barbed remark. Kent was especially nice to Peggy Sue. What was it about this overweight, stupid woman that attracted men? Grandma seemed to be taken by her too. *Am I jealous? No, of course not. How could anyone with a smidgen of sense be jealous of the likes of Peggy Sue?*

Chapter Seven

June 18, 1945
Monday Afternoon

The bus pulled into the Houston station at eleven-thirty am, thirty minutes past its due date. Kent was on his feet before it came to a halt. He stepped back to give Sara room to move to the aisle. As they descended the steps a dignified older woman and a balding, portly man rushed toward them. A cigar hung from one side of the man's mouth. The woman wore glasses and what Sara took to be a superior expression.

"Mother, Father!" Kent grabbed them both in a hug.

Mother and Father? He called his parents Mother and Father? Sara thought that was only in the movies. Her heart fell to the pit of her stomach.

Kent stepped back and put his arm around her waist. "I want you to meet Sara, my wife."

Sara extended her right hand to Mrs. Holden. "How do you do, Mrs. Holden." Kent certainly didn't look like his mama.

"I am well, thank you, my dear." She shook Sara's hand. "I trust you had a pleasant trip."

"Yes, ma'am, it was very pleasant." Sara extended her hand to Mr. Holden. "How do you do, sir?" He doesn't look much like his daddy either.

"I'm fine as frog's hair." Mr. Holden pumped her hand. "My, you are a little thing." Before Sara could think of a response to that remark, he turned to Kent. "Give me your baggage stubs. I'll collect your suitcases."

"We will be waiting for you at the car," Mrs. Holden said, as she motioned for Sara and Kent to follow her. "And don't dilly-dally. It's hot out here."

She led them to a black Chrysler Imperial sedan. Sara had never before seen such a fine automobile. It must have cost a mint.

Mr. Holden soon appeared with a suitcase in each hand, and a third one tucked under his arm. He had slung Kent's duffle bag over his shoulder. He set them on the ground, fished in his pockets, and took out his car keys. "Lordy, it's hot in that station."

"Stop talking and get these bags loaded." Mrs. Holden fanned her gloved hand in front of her face. "Honestly, Lester. You're as slow as the seven-year itch."

"Keep your shirt on, Martha." Lester unlocked the trunk, put the bags inside and slammed the lid down hard.

Sara wondered why Martha wore gloves and a hat in weather such as this. She stole a look in Kent's direction.

He winked one eye and smiled.

Kent helped Sara into the back seat and was set to help his mother into the front.

"Put Mother in the back seat." Lester pulled a fresh cigar from his shirt pocket, and bit off the end. "She's a back-seat driver. She may as well ride back there."

"Whatever you say."

After Sara slid across the soft beige upholstery to the other side of the car, Martha got in beside her. "Somebody needs to help you." She put her purse on the floorboard and removed her gloves before turning toward Sara. "Lester is the worst driver in the state of Texas, maybe in the entire USA."

"Nothing much has changed around here, I see." Kent rolled his window glass down. "You do have a new car."

"Roll up that glass." Martha put her hands on her head. "The wind is ruining my hairdo."

"Put your hat on." Kent scooted down in his seat.

"You haven't changed either. You're as sassy and smart-mouthed as you were when you marched off to war." Once more she turned toward Sara. "Maybe you can make him behave. I never could. Ariel didn't even try. She was as wild as he was. Cynthia did her best, for all the good it did her. He up and left her. She was broken-hearted. She still is. I tell her all the time—"

Kent interrupted, "Mother, please. Sara isn't interested in hearing about my two biggest mistakes."

"Let the boy alone, Mother. He's been through a lot in the last four years." Lester shifted his unlit cigar to the other side of his mouth. "Yes siree, my son is a genuine, bona fide war hero."

"Tonight, we will honor him," Martha announced. Pride vibrated through her voice. Once more she turned and addressed Sara. "I'm depending on you, my dear, to keep him in line."

"I don't think Kent needs –" Sara was at a loss for words.

Kent turned toward the back seat. "Mother, you shouldn't have planned a soiree without consulting me first."

"It's a surprise soiree, or it was until now."

"Martha, you never told me about no soiree." Lester turned off the highway and into a fashionable neighborhood.

Sara stared out the window at the palatial homes that sat far back from the tree-lined avenue. *And I worried about what Kent would think of my family.* Words she had often heard Grandma advocate, ran through her mind like a malediction. *When you marry a man, you marry the entire family. Better have a good look at them before you say I do.*

"We're home, y'all." Lester pulled into the driveway of a palatial three-story brick home.

The nagging bud of uneasiness that sprouted inside Sara the moment she saw Kent's parents bloomed now into full-blown fear.

"Izzie should have lunch on the table." Martha reached for her purse. "I told Mrs. MacNay to prepare something light since I will be serving a buffet supper around seven o'clock this evening."

"Anything Miz Mac makes is fine with me. That woman is some cook." Lester helped his wife from the car.

Kent opened the car door for Sara, and helped her onto the driveway.

She smiled up at him and murmured, "Don't leave me."

"Never, my darling, not in a million years." He put his arm around her waist, and pulled her close before whispering in her ear, "Sorry about the soiree."

"It's all right." It was not, not really. Why didn't Kent tell her his parents were so well-to-do? And what in the world was a soiree?

June 18, 1945
Monday Evening

Sara sat on a chair in the corner of the sitting room of the suite Martha assigned to her and Kent. Being on the third floor of this huge house was not to her liking. What would she do if this place caught fire? She looked around at the elegant furnishings, heavy brocade curtains, and the thick carpets. It would spread like a grass fire.

"I don't know if I can do this." The nearer it came time to go downstairs, the more anxious Sara became. "I have never been to a soiree. I'm not even sure what that is."

"Don't worry about it." Kent came from the bedroom. How elegant he looked in his uniform, with all his medals pinned to his chest. "It's Mother's word for a party. Since I can remember, she has loved to put on airs. Father's business success has provided the money for her to break into Houston society's upper crust."

"Why didn't you tell me your parents were wealthy?" Sara had sworn not to ask that question. It was out of her mouth before she could stop it.

Kent stood in the middle of the floor with his hands in his pockets, staring up at the nine-foot ceiling. "They are newly-rich. When I left in November of 1940 to join my division, they were dirt-poor. My esteemed father owned a junk yard. He made what little money he got together selling used car parts." Her husband came to sit on the bed, and patted the spot beside him. "Come over here by me." Sara moved to sit by his side.

He put his arms around her, and drew her close to him. "When car manufacturers stopped making automobiles to build trucks and tanks for the war, Father saw his chance. He jacked up his prices. He began repairing cars and charging exorbitant fees for parts. He got into the salvage business. When he had the opportunity to buy a bankrupt automobile agency, he jumped at the chance."

"Why would he do that?" Sara pushed back and stared up into her husband's face. "It's been four years since a U.S. manufacturer made a car."

"They will start up again. Father saw that. He could also see his salvage and used-parts business coming to an end." Kent kissed the tip of her nose. "We should skip Mother's soiree and stay here." Pulling her near, he kissed her passionately.

Sara gave herself over to the bliss of his embrace.

A loud knock on the door made her pull back.

"Kent, open the door."

Kent lifted his head. "Go away, Mother."

"Guests are arriving." Martha turned the knob of the locked door and banged on it when she was denied entrance. "Cynthia is here. She's looking forward to seeing you."

Cynthia? A chill ran down Sara's backbone.

"Mother, please don't tell me you invited one of my ex-wives to your *soiree*." Kent made 'soiree' sound like a swearword.

Martha's pleading voice sounded from the other side of the door. "Don't spoil your welcome home soiree by complaining about my guest list."

"I should have known." Kent shook his head. "Did you invite Ariel too?" He stood and heaved a weary sigh. "Tell me, did you?"

"This is an RSVP affair. Ariel didn't respond to my invitation, but knowing Ariel as I do, there is no guarantee she won't be here. Are you coming downstairs or aren't you?"

Sara's temper ignited.

"We will be down soon." She reined in her exploding anger. It seemed she had a mother-in-law who was set on causing trouble between her and her husband. She stood and extended her hand in Kent's direction. "Are you ready?"

"You look beautiful." Kent pulled her into his arms, and once more kissed her. Sara kissed him back. As he released her, she heard footsteps going down the stairs.

Chapter Eight

June 19, 1945
Tuesday Morning

Sara awoke with an aching head. She turned to stare at the man sleeping beside her as memories of last night's dreadful soiree hopped into her mind.

The entire evening was a nightmare. Before she stepped off the last stair riser and into the palatial room, she knew it was going to be. The guests were dressed in formal wear, the men wore tuxedos, and the women had on long, elegant evening dresses. Sara wore her knee-length, one-and-only little black dress. She clutched Kent's arm. "Why didn't you tell me?"

"I didn't know." He was set to say more when they were accosted by a tall, slender woman with flaming red hair. She wore a green sequined gown that fit her flawless figure like a second skin.

"Darling, it's so good to see you again." She threw her arms around Kent and hugged him.

He kissed her on the cheek and began a hasty introduction. "Sara, this is—"

"Never mind. I know who she is." Sara extended her right hand. "Hello, Cynthia."

"Hello." Cynthia shook Sara's hand as she gave her a head-to-toe scan. "Robbing the cradle these days, Kent?"

"Does that bother you?" Sara moved nearer her husband. "Don't let it, because it doesn't concern you."

Anger smoldered in the green of Cynthia's eyes. Her jaw tightened and then relaxed. "Your little kitten has claws." She hugged Kent again, before walking away with her head held high.

"Sara, you surprised me." Kent took her hand. "You surprised Cynthia, too. She didn't expect such a direct attack. The truth is, neither did I." He led her toward the crowd of guests. "Let's say our hellos and goodbyes and get out of here."

Good thought, but it was not that simple. Before Sara could collect her wits, Martha had them in a reception line. "Never mind eating just now. We must meet and greet before the entertainment starts."

"Don't tell me Gwendolyn Wingate is going to sing." Kent grimaced.

"Of course not." Martha patted his arm, making him frown. "Dear Gwendolyn departed this vale of tears last year. We are privileged to have Amelia Winchester with us tonight."

After enduring a too-long reception line of limp handshakes and halfhearted greetings, Martha herded her charges to the front row of chairs that were placed around a grand piano.

Kent helped Sara into her chair and then sat beside her before leaning over to whisper in her ear. "Prepare yourself. It's going to be a long evening."

Sara shushed him. "She is doing this for you."

"My wife is both generous and naïve."

Martha stepped forward with Amelia Winchester in tow and began her glowing introduction. Amelia was a stocky little middle-aged woman with a somewhat square head, huge round eyes, and almost no neck. Little tufts of hair covered her ears.

Sara leaned toward Kent and whispered, "Matilda looks like a screech owl."

He whispered back, "Let's hope she doesn't sound like one."

The accompanist began to play and Sara sank into reverie. Once two screech owls built a nest in the hollow of a stump near the well house. Each night she listened for the toot, toot, toot, toot, toot, sometimes followed with a trill not unlike that of a song bird. A wave of homesickness washed over her. She wanted to go home. She didn't belong here.

Sara shook her head, sat up and pushed her pillow behind her back as she was jerked from a bad recollection back to the present.

"Bad dream?" Kent opened his eyes and smiled at her. "Good morning, sweetheart, if you are still my sweetheart. Sorry about last night."

"Forget last night. It wasn't your fault." How could she blame him for something that wasn't his doing? "I will never go to another one of your mother's soirees."

"Is that a promise?" His smile boosted her spirits.

"It is." Sara lifted her right hand. "Scout's honor."

"Were you a girl scout?" He raised on his elbow and put his chin in his hand. "You could have fooled me."

"I wasn't a girl scout." This man could charm the birds right out of the trees. "That's what James and I always said to each other when we made a solemn promise."

"James was a boy scout?"

Sara laughed aloud. "No."

Kent pulled her into his arms. "Forget about James. Forget about scouts, boy or girl. Forget Mother's terrible welcome home party." He kissed her until she was breathless, and then lifted his head to stare into her eyes. "I love you, my darling."

"I love you too, so much." She gave herself over to her husband's sweet lovemaking.

Later they went downstairs for breakfast. After that Lester insisted Kent come with him to the car dealership.

They were scarcely out the door before Martha asked, "Would you like to see pictures of Kent when he was little?"

"Oh, yes, I would."

"I'll have to fetch the albums."

Sara sat at the dining room table and waited for Martha's return. Pictures of Kent when he was a baby? Maybe she had misjudged Martha.

She returned carrying a picture album under each arm. "He was such a darling little boy, but stubborn. And willful at times."

She sat beside Sara, opened an album, and pointed to the picture of a small child riding a tricycle. "That's Kent when he was three-years-old. Isn't he adorable?"

He was, and Sara said so. It occurred to her, quite suddenly, that she had no idea when Kent's birthday was. She was set to ask, and thought better of it.

Martha turned a page. "Will you look at this? He was such a precious child, even then."

Sara looked. What she saw was the photograph of a tiny ragtag little boy with a smudged face and in dire need of a haircut.

"That's the way the poor child looked when we first got him." Martha rubbed her fingers across the picture. "I fell in love with him at first glance."

"That is Kent? You're not his birth mother?" The words were out before Sara could stop them.

"Of course not, dear. I can't have children. At first Lester was so disappointed. Then one day he came home from work and said to me, 'Martha, I have found a little boy who needs a mother as badly as you need a son.' I laughed. Who in their right mind would give away a child? I forgot the matter, but you know Lester. What he wants, he finds a way to get. One afternoon a few weeks later, he took me to meet Kent. The poor little thing's mother was dying. A neighbor was caring for him. For me, it was love at first sight. I said, then and there, 'I'm going to adopt this little boy' and I did."

"He's adopted?"

"Of course, he is. Stop asking silly questions and look at this picture. It's an absolutely charming snapshot of Kent when he was four years old." This was crazy. Why hadn't Kent told her?

Chapter Nine

June 19, 1945
Tuesday Afternoon

It was well into the afternoon before Sara got Kent alone. She closed the door to their suite, locked it, and turned to face him. "Make yourself comfortable. We have things to talk about and some decisions to make."

"Come and snuggle with me." Kent sat on one end of the couch and patted the cushion beside him.

"Not now, not yet." If she got too close to him, they would end up in bed with nothing settled. "This morning your mother showed me pictures of you when you were a little boy. Why didn't you tell me you were adopted?"

"I didn't think it made any difference. Does it?" His voice was harsh, his brown eyes stony.

"No, not one bit." She had hit a nerve. She should have been more tactful. She would be next time. "I was just curious, but that's not what I want to talk about. We need to make plans for our future."

"I thought we'd spend the remainder of the week with Mother and Father." Kent stretched his legs in front of him and stared at the toes of his shoes. "Mother wants us to attend church with her next Sunday. I said we had other plans." After a pause, he asked, "Should I have asked you before refusing her invitation?"

"I wish you had. I think we should go. Attending church is important to me."

"How important?"

"Very important, but that's not what I want to discuss." How could she say this tactfully? Maybe she couldn't; nevertheless, it must be said. "I want us to make solid, long-range goals and set some concrete plans about our future."

"Like what?" Kent asked.

"Like where are we going to live? Like what will we do for a living? Do you want to go back to the farm?"

"Is that what you want?"

"That's one of the things we must talk about. I want to be where you are, but I—"

He jumped to his feet, rushed to her side, took her in his arms and danced her around the room. "I was hoping that would be your answer. Thank you, my darling, thank you, thank you, thank you."

He drew her into an intimate embrace, and kissed her, gently at first, and then with more and more fervor.

She melted into his arms, losing herself in the magic of his touch.

After long moments of bliss, Kent broke the embrace, leaned back and smiled into her eyes. "I am so glad you don't want to go back to that farm." He rested his chin atop of her head. "I'm not a farmer. I don't think I ever could be."

"That's not what—" Sara reined in her tongue. "It's not—once more, she stopped the words that stirred in her muddled brain before they could escape through her mouth.

Kent led her to the couch, and sat beside her. "I am going to make you so happy. Father has made me a partner in his car dealership. I know how hard you worked on that farm. You will never have to work that hard again. I am going to—"

She stopped him by laying her finger across his lips. "Shouldn't you be saying *we* are going to?"

"I got carried away." He took her hand in his and kissed her fingertips. His expression grew serious. "I have wasted so much of my life behaving like a juvenile delinquent. Four years of war made me grow up. Now all I want is a home and a stable, peaceful life. I want you to be the queen of my home. I love you, Sara."

His sweet words melted her heart. Gone were any thoughts of objecting to his plans. "Tell me more about our home and our family."

"You and I are our family." He hugged her and then released her. "I don't want children."

"Why not?" His words cut through Sara like a rusty knife.

"I have my reasons." He stood and rammed his hands into his pockets. His face set in hard lines. "One of them is, I know nothing about my birth parents."

"I always dreamed of being a mother." This was a Kent she didn't know. "Not knowing about your birth parents means nothing to me."

"On this one subject there is no compromise. Sorry, Sara, but that's the way it is." He sat beside her once again. "Mother says we can stay here as long as we want, but I think we should find an apartment as soon as possible." He tagged his statement with a cautious, "What do you think?"

She thought she had to change his mind about not wanting children. She said, "I lived in an apartment in Orange. I didn't like sharing the walls of my home with strangers."

"Had you rather have a house?" Kent asked.

"Maybe we can find a nice little bungalow on the outskirts of town."

"Then a house it will be. Maybe we can find something with a picket fence around it. Why don't we enjoy this week with my parents and talk again next Sunday?"

"I had rather find a home of our own as soon as possible." Sara stood and walked across the room before turning. "I'm not comfortable here."

Kent was on his feet and coming toward her. "Has someone here said or done something to offend you?" He stopped directly in front of her, put his hands on her shoulders and looked into her eyes.

"It's nothing like that." She took one of his hands from her shoulder and led him back to the couch. "Sit down, and I will try to explain."

"Does this have something to do with Cynthia?" He stood, staring down at her. "She means nothing to me. Our marriage was Mother's idea."

"It's not about Cynthia." Annoyance put a snap in Sara's voice. "Will you please sit down?"

He sat, but most reluctantly.

"I love you, Kent, but sometimes I don't know you very well." She waited for some reply. When she became aware that she was not going to get one, she sighed and continued. "Your world is one I don't know. I'm a country girl."

"You're my girl." He put his arms around her. "You're my frightened little girl. You don't have to be. You have me to protect you."

"You can't protect me from myself." What she felt was not fright, but disappointment. She wanted a family. Kent didn't. *I will change his mind.*

"Oh, my darling." He lifted her chin until she was staring into his eyes. "You are a riddle entwined in an enigma."

He kissed her and she felt that same old magic his touch always brought.

She loved him and he loved her. *Dear God, please let that be enough.*

Chapter Ten

June 20, 1945
Wednesday Morning

When Sara awoke, Kent was not in bed. He left a note tucked in one side of the dressing table mirror in the bathroom. It read:

My Darling,
Father needs me to help him with getting the partnership papers drawn up and notarized today. A relator, his name is Pete Graves, will call for you at one o'clock. He will show you some houses. Choose the one you like best.
I will see you at dinner time.
Your loving husband,
Kent

Sara didn't know if she should be angry or hurt. She was a little of both. *He promised.* Quick hindsight brought to her mind he hadn't promised anything, except to be sure she went house hunting today.

As she dressed her anger cooled. Kent had a job now. His father had graciously given him a partnership in a thriving business. She was being petty and ungrateful. She went downstairs to find Martha sitting at the dining room table nursing a cup of coffee. "Good morning, Mrs. Holden."

Martha snapped, "What's good about it?"

"Have I done something to displease you?" Sara sat in a chair across from her mother-in-law.

"Lester and I open our home to you and you refuse out hospitality."

"Kent and I appreciate your offer. We are grateful for your kindness, but—"

"Don't blame Kent for this foolish decision. He would go to live in the Arctic if he thought that was what you wanted." Martha blew out a long breath and took a sip of coffee. "He's more smitten with you than he ever was with Ariel. Imagine a man his age acting like a lovesick teenager. It won't last. It never does with Kent."

Sara was at a loss for words. Before she could form a response, Mrs. MacNay appeared carrying a tray. She was a middle aged, ample-figured woman. Her graying hair was pulled back into a bun at the nape of her neck. "I brought your breakfast." She paused and shook her head. "Two Mrs. Holdens won't do." She set the tray in front of Sara. "What am I supposed to call you?"

Sara stared down at the plate of eggs, biscuits, and sausages. There was also a cup of steaming coffee and a glass of orange juice. The food looked delicious and smelled heavenly. "You can call me Sara."

"Is that all right with you, Mrs. Holden?" Mrs. MacNay put her hands in her apron pockets and waited for Martha's answer.

After a spate of silence, Martha replied, "Miss Sara is acceptable. It is not appropriate for you to call my son's wife only by her Christian name."

Her overbearing mother-in-law may control everybody and everything else in this household, but the name Sara chose for Mrs. MacNay to call her was none of Martha's business. "My name is Sara, Mrs. MacNay. That is what you will call me if you expect me to answer. The subject is closed."

"May I go now, Mrs. Holden?" Mrs. MacNay inched toward the door.

"Yes, please do." Martha waved one hand in the direction of the kitchen. She turned on Sara with fire in her eyes. "How dare you disrespect me in the presence of the hired help?"

It was on the tip of Sara's tongue to let go with a scathing reply. She thought twice and kept her mouth shut.

"Cat got your tongue?" Martha folded her arms across her breasts and waited.

In her most conciliatory voice Sara said, "I did not disrespect you. I disagreed with you. There is a difference. If I offended you, it was not intentional." *Don't expect me to say I'm sorry, because I'm not.*

Martha burst into tears. "I had so hoped you would be like Cynthia, but I fear you are a carbon copy of Ariel, except for your looks." She sniffed and wiped her eyes with a napkin. "Ariel has blond hair. She is tall and very curvy."

Since she was a teenager, Sara had been self-conscious about her height, or lack of it. Being reminded of that deficiency, on the heels of being compared unfavorably to Kent's two first wives, left her with burning cheeks and a taste of humiliation on her tongue.

Izzie came through the kitchen door. "Mrs. MacNay sent me to ask what she should make for dinner. I mean for lunch."

"Something light and no dessert." Martha dried her eyes on her napkin. "Try to remember, dear, that the noon meal is called lunch."

"Yes, ma'am. Can I go now?"

"Not can I, may I. Yes, you may."

Izzie scurried back through the swinging door that separated the dining room from the kitchen.

"That girl will be the death of me." Martha laid her napkin on the table. "Why is life so hard?"

"How old is Izzie?" Sara had to ask. She looked about fifteen. Why would a pretty, scared little fifteen-year-old be working as a maid?

"She's nineteen." Martha shrugged, and resumed complaining about her difficult life. "I try to teach her manners and etiquette, but all in vain. Lester says I am too good for my own good, being so nice to people. I can't help it. That's just my nature."

This woman was delusional, and Lester was either crazy or a big liar. Sara excused herself and made a hasty retreat. She was halfway up the second flight of stairs before she realized she didn't eat her breakfast. Was the hope of enjoying a good meal worth the risk of having to cope with her mother-in-law again? She decided it wasn't and continued to climb the stairs.

She was scarcely in her sitting room when Izzie knocked on the door. "It's me, Miss Sara. I brought your breakfast."

"Please, come in."

"I can't turn the knob. I'm carrying your tray."

Sara hurried to open the door.

Izzie entered, sat the tray on a table, and turned to go without speaking another word.

"Wait," Sara called after her. "Don't go. Sit down."

"I have work to do." Izzie turned to face Sara. "Mrs. Holden complains when I dilly-dally around. Whatever that means."

It meant Mrs. Holden was a tyrant. "I never knew anyone named Izzie before." Sara sat, hoping Izzie would follow suit.

She didn't. Neither did she make for the exit. "That's really not my name. Mama named me Elizabeth after Princess Elizabeth. My little sister couldn't say Elizabeth. Mama told her to call me Lizzie. She couldn't say that either. She could say Izzie, so that got to be what everybody called me. Can I go now?" Without waiting for an answer, she sped away.

Sara ate her cold breakfast.

Chapter Eleven

June 20, 1945
Wednesday Afternoon

Pete Graves arrived promptly at one o'clock. Sara waited for him in the foyer. The moment the doorbell rang, she answered. The tall man who stood on the other side of the screen could have been the scarecrow from The Wizard of Oz. "Mrs. Holden?" He tipped his hat revealing a mop of yellow straw-like hair.
Sara stepped onto the porch. "I'm ready." She extended her hand. "I'm Sara."
"Call me Pete." He stretched one long, skinny arm in her direction. His shirt sleeve pulled half-way up to his elbow.
They were in Pete's car and almost to the highway before either of them spoke again. Sara broke the silence. "I prefer a house that is out of town. I'd like room for a garden, and maybe a few chickens."
"I don't have anything like that right now. I don't expect I will have anyway soon." Pete slowed for a stop sign. "There's a housing shortage, in case you didn't know." He drove through the intersection and turned south onto the highway. "The best I can offer is an apartment that should be available in six months."
His words hit her like a bucket of cold water. She did know there was a housing shortage. She had no idea it was so acute. "I don't want to live in an apartment."
"I can show you a house in a suburban housing development. It's called Sunny Acres. A lot of vets and their families are buying houses there. Veterans can get a G.I loan. You can get into one of them in three to four months, if you're lucky. I'm headed that way now."
"It can't hurt to look." Sara stared at the passing scenery as she listened to Sam's sales pitch.
"These houses are landscaped when you buy them. Trees and rosebushes are already planted. There's an attached garage." He pulled off the highway and traveled down a dirt road for a few miles. "Attached garages are the latest things.

You can drive into your garage, get out, and go into your home without going outside. Think how nice that will be when it rains."

"When it rains, I doubt we could get down this dirt road to get home."

Pete waved one hand in the air. "The county will pave this road."

"When?" Sara asked.

"Sooner or later." He turned into a subdivision with narrow streets lined on either side with tiny box-like houses. Children played in yards. A woman stood on her stoop. She waved as they drove by.

"This is a nice neighborhood." Pete pointed to the woman. "Lots of friendly people live here."

"The lots are so narrow," Sara complained. "The houses all look the same. I suppose I could fence the back yard, and have a garden there."

"No fences allowed." Pete stopped before a house with a sign in front that read, Model Home. "You can look at the model and tell me what you think."

"I don't have to look to know what I think. I don't want to live here." Sara reconsidered her options. "Maybe I will have a look at an apartment." Anything would be better than this.

"If that's what you want." Pete made a U-turn in the middle of the street. "I know women who would give their eye teeth for a nice little home out here." He hummed under his breath as he drove onto the dirt road.

Sara asked, "Where is this apartment located?"

Pete stopped his humming, turned, and smiled in her direction. "A nice two-bedroom flat will soon be available. It's in an apartment house near Kent's business."

"What do you call soon?"

"Four to six months." Pete pulled on to the highway and increased his speed.

"Do you know my husband?" Sara turned in her seat and stared at him.

"I'm acquainted with him." Pete shrugged. "Lester is a good friend of mine. He sold me this car I'm driving. Do you want to see the apartment?"

Sara did and she said so.

It was a decision she repented of later. It was on a street congested with traffic. The apartment was tiny and cramped. Sounds from outside came through the walls. It was on the third floor. There was no elevator.

As they got back into Pete's car, he asked, "What did you think of the place?"

"I would suffocate if I had to live there, if the outside noises didn't drive me crazy first."

"You would get used to the noise." Pete pulled out of the drive and into the flow of traffic. "Would you like to look at another subdivision?"

"Take me home." What she wouldn't give for fresh country air to breathe and some space to move around in.

"I'll keep you in mind. If I find something I think you would like, I'll call you."

"Thank you, Pete."

Martha met Sara at the door. "Your mother called. She left a message."

A dozen dreaded thoughts crowded into Sara's mind. Did Grandma have another heart attack? Was Daddy worse? Had something happened to James? "Tell me quickly, what did she say?"

"Goodness me, I don't answer the telephone. You will have to ask Mrs. Mac-Nay." Martha closed the front door. "I must get back to making my list." She left without further ado.

By the time Sara reached the kitchen she was frantic. She pushed through the swinging door. "What was my mama's message?"

"She wants you to call her." Mrs. MacNay turned from the stove.

"Did she say why?"

"Calm down." Mrs. MacNay looked around the room before lowering her voice. "She says not to worry. Nothing bad has happened. She's anxious about you. She hasn't heard a word from you since you left home last Monday."

"I said I'd call Jenkin's Grocery the moment I got here and tell her I arrived safely. I forgot." Sara pulled a chair from under the kitchen table and sat down. "How could I have been so remiss?"

"Don't you fret. Your mama understands. I'm making a banana pudding. Mr. Holden does love his sweets." Mrs. MacNay turned off the burner, and removed her pan from the stove." Would you like a glass of iced tea?"

"I would love a glass of tea, but first I have to call Mr. Jenkins and ask him to tell Mama I'm okay."

"I already told your mama you're fine." Mrs. MacNay took a pitcher of iced tea from the refrigerator. "She said to tell you to write her a letter." She grasped two glasses from a shelf and came toward the table. "Did you find a house to your liking?" She sat the pitcher and the glasses in front of Sara. "Help yourself."

"No. I didn't realize houses were so scarce." Sara filled her glass to the brim

"Everything's scarce these days." Mrs. MacNay sat and poured tea into her glass. "Maybe things will get better now that the war is over."

"At least all our soldier boys are back home." Sara took a long sip of tea and let the cold liquid slide down her throat.

"Not all of them. My son Willie was killed at the battle of Guadalcanal in 1943."

"I'm so sorry."

"It's all right." Mrs. MacNay's eyes filled with tears.

"It's not all right." How could she be so insensitive? "I made you cry and I'm sorry. She reached across the table and caught Mrs. Mac Nay's wrist.

"I always cry when I think about Willie." Mrs. MacNay gave Sara's hand a gentle squeeze. "He was so young, only twenty-one years old. It seems like such a waste. He was a good Christian boy. I have the comfort of knowing he's with Jesus now. He will never have to suffer again." She stood. "I have to get supper ready. Mr. Holden will be home soon. He comes through the door hungry as a wolf." She lifted her voice several decibels. "Izzieee! Get in here. We got things to do."

Sara said goodbye and left. She took her tea and retreated to her quarters.

Chapter Twelve

June 20, 1945
Wednesday Evening

Lester pushed his plate aside. "That was the best steak I ever tasted."

Martha's fork stopped midway to her mouth. "It's good you enjoyed it because we don't have any meat stamps left for the rest of this month." She turned to Sara. "Did you bring your ration book?" Before Sara could reply, she questioned Kent. "Did you apply for your ration books?"

She shook her fork in Lester's direction. "You will be singing another tune when you have macaroni and cheese for dinner three evenings in a row before we switch to Spam."

"I like macaroni and cheese." Lester reached in his shirt pocket for a cigar. "I can stomach Spam for a few days, but don't put any more of that terrible striped margarine on my table ever again."

"I have my ration book." Sara broke into her in-laws' conversation.

"Mother." Kent reached across the table and tapped the back of Martha's hand. "I have my ration books. Settle down and enjoy your dinner."

Izzie appeared carrying a large dish of banana pudding. "Here's your pudding, Mr. Holden. It's just like you ordered, with no meringue on top." She set the dish in front of Lester and hurried back to the kitchen.

"Lester, how could you." A thunder cloud of a frown creased Martha's face. "Now there will be no sugar for our coffee or our iced tea. We will have to use saccharine. You know how I hate that stuff."

"I get hungry for something sweet." Lester laid his unlit cigar aside and pulled his plate back to him. "I work hard. I need my nourishment." He spooned a heaping serving of pudding into his plate.

"Izzie didn't bring dessert dishes." Martha raised both hands in disgust. "How crude." She shouted, "Izzie!"

Izzie appeared carrying dessert dishes and set them beside the pudding. "I forgot."

"That's all right, dear," Martha said. "Please try to remember next time."

"Yes, ma'am, Mrs. Holden." Izzie vanished as quickly as she had appeared.

Lester ate his pudding with great gusto.

Martha shouted, "Lester."

He stopped and looked up. "What now?"

"Don't be uncouth. Put your pudding in your dessert dish."

"Ah, Martha, do I have to?"

"You most assuredly do." Martha laid one hand across her chest. "I insist on civility and good manners at my table."

"All right." Lester raked the remainder of his pudding into a dessert dish. "I want you to know I do this under protest."

June 20, 1945
Wednesday Night

"Alone at last." Kent sat on the side of the bed and began the process of removing his shoes. "I thought about you all day. I counted the minutes until I could get back to you."

"I missed you, too." Sara sat at the dressing table, brushing her long hair.

"You have no idea how beautiful you are." Kent removed his socks and pushed them into his shoes. "I love the way your hair falls in waves down your back." He pushed his shoes under the bed. "I talked to Pete late this afternoon. He said you didn't like the house or the apartment he showed you. He also told me he doubted you would ever find what you are looking for."

"Even if I did, it would be months before we could move into a place of our own." Sara turned. "I had no idea there was such a housing shortage."

"Come and sit by me." Kent extended one hand. "We will eventually get a house of our own. Until then, we have a roof over our head. That's something."

Sara didn't look forward to an extended stay with her in-laws, but it seemed she had no choice. She would make a concentrated effort to get along with Martha. She was Kent's mother, sort of.

"If the mountain won't come to Mohammed," Kent stood and removed his shirt. "Mohammed must go to the mountain." He came across the room and sat beside her. "I love you, sweet Sara."

"I love you, too. You don't know how much." That old enchantment she knew so well swept her away on wings of passion. Nothing else mattered, not children, not houses, or apartments, not even living for a while with quirky in-laws. She lost herself in the thrill of his kiss.

June 21, 1945
Thursday

Thursday morning Sara wrote Mama a long letter and spent the remainder of the day reading *A Tree Grows in Brooklyn.* Izzie brought her breakfast and lunch, and put her letter in the mailbox.

That evening, over dinner, Martha complained to Kent that his wife was anti-social.

"Sorry about that." Kent smiled and shrugged.

"Let the girl alone, Martha," Lester said between bites. "If you gotta run your mouth, talk to Mrs. Mac or Izzie."

"You have no respect for me, Lester, no respect whatsoever." Martha burst into tears.

"Oh, no." Lester was immediately contrite. He got up from his chair and moved to stand by Martha's side. "Darlin' you know I would never do something to hurt you."

"I do not converse on a social level with the hired help." Martha dried her tears with a napkin. "They arc not my equals."

"I clean forgot. I apologize. Do you forgive me?" Lester patted his wife's shoulder.

"Of course, I do. Sit down and finish your meal."

Lester moved back to his chair, sat down, and once more tackled his food with enthusiasm.

If Sara lived to be a hundred, she would never understand Kent's parents. She took a bite of her Spam. Mrs. Mac had baked it in an orange glaze and seasoned it with cloves and pineapple slices. It was very good and she said so.

Martha responded with, "The food served at my table is always appetizing."

Lester who was either fearless or stupid, added, "As long as you hang onto Mrs. Mac. You can't boil water without scorching it." Sara immediately dismissed stupid. Lester was a lot of things—shrewd, calculating, maybe even devious, but never stupid. She knew she couldn't spend all day tomorrow in this house.

"I am going shopping tomorrow for a nice dress to wear to church Sunday." She breathed a sigh of relief, thinking she had found a way to escape.

"What a wonderful idea." Martha clapped her hands together. "I know a lovely little tea room where we can have lunch."

"I'll send a car and driver to cart the two of you around town." Lester slapped the table with his open hand. "By Jove, Sara girl. That's a fine idea."

Sara looked at Kent, hoping he would come to her rescue. He didn't seem to recognize she had a problem. "I insist, darling, that you buy several dresses, and anything else you need." He laid his hand over hers. "You will have Mother to show you around. Father is right, the two of you should have a grand time."

"Yes. A grand time." Sara realized when to accept defeat. She would rather face Chinese water torture than spend the day shopping with her mother-in-law.

Chapter Thirteen

Sara was awakened by a rap on the door. She sat up. "Yes, who is it?"

Izzie's voice called from the other side. "Mrs. Holden says it's time to get up and get ready for church. She says for Mr. Kent to wear his uniform and all his medals."

Kent rolled over and yawned. "I hear you. Run along now." He smiled at Sara. "Put on that new dress you bought. I want to see you in it."

"I bought new shoes, too. They are white and have four-inch heels and peep toes." She'd spent her last shoe coupon. She would be tall. Maybe not tall, but taller. Sara went toward the bathroom.

Kent called after her. "Did you enjoy shopping with Mother?"

"Things were a little difficult at first." Much to her surprise, the day she spent with Martha was not all that bad. "There were a few difficult moments. When your mother finally recognized I was going to choose my own dress, things went more smoothly."

Sara took a leisurely bath. She had always, before coming to the Holdens, bathed in a number three wash tub, or showered in an outside makeshift cold-water shower. Living in this place had its compensations.

She dried, put on her underwear, and her new dress. It was red with white polka dots, knee-length with a V-neckline, short sleeves, and a gored skirt. Sara thought it was beautiful.

Unfortunately, her mother-in-law didn't agree. When Sara stepped from the dressing room, wearing what she thought was a lovely creation, Martha splayed her hand over her heart. "It's too long and it's red. Find something more appropriate for a young woman of your station in life."

Sara wasn't sure what her station in life was. She didn't argue. She did buy the dress.

Martha conceded defeat, but most ungraciously. "I hope they do alterations here. I'll inquire."

Sara assured her there was no need. She could do her own alterations, since they amounted to no more than putting a wider hem in her skirt.

Then came the battle over Sara buying a bag, a hat, and gloves to match her shoes. After some harangue, they compromised on a white straw bonnet with a semi-deep crown and a narrow brim.

When Martha chose a white square straw bag with an elaborate clasp, Sara agreed. She asked Martha to choose her gloves, which the other woman readily did. "These are perfect, dear." She held up a pair of white lace gloves.

Sara didn't object. By that time, she would have agreed to a pair of woolen mittens.

"Ta da." Sara stepped from the bathroom into the bedroom wearing her new dress and her new shoes. She crossed her fingers and waited for her husband's reaction.

"You're beautiful." Kent's eyes sparkled as he surveyed her from head to toe. "Absolutely beautiful."

"I would have liked for the belt to be wider, but according to government restrictions on belt widths, this is the limit."

"No." Kent held up one hand. "The dress is perfect. I wouldn't change one thing." He wore a white shirt and a multi-striped tie. His trousers were navy blue with wide cuffs. His feet were shod in black wing-tipped shoes. He was so handsome that he took her breath away.

"Your mother will be disappointed that you aren't wearing your uniform."

"Mother will cool down, but the weather won't. It will only get hotter." Kent grabbed his pork-pie straw hat, set it on his head, and gave the crown a little thump. "Are you ready?" He offered her his arm.

Sara took it and smiled up at him. Happiness sang through her veins until she remembered what Kent had said about not wanting children. She pushed that thought aside. She would change his mind. All she needed was a little time.

The church was in the heart of the city. It was a huge cathedral-like building with a bell tower rising high over the front entrance. Sara stared in awe. She had never seen a church so fine, except in pictures. What a magnificent structure.

Lester grumbled as he searched for a parking place. "I knew we were going to be too late to find a decent place to park."

"It's Kent's fault." Martha leaned from the back seat and punched Kent on his shoulder. "If you hadn't been so stubborn about wearing your uniform, we would have been here thirty minutes ago."

"You know how hard-headed the boy is. Why did you keep nagging him?" Lester wheeled into a vacant parking space across the street from the church. "The two of you argued for thirty minutes. He still ain't wearing a uniform or medals."

"It's too hot to get dressed up in that uniform." Kent got out of the car and opened the door for his mother.

"Thank heavens we have a reserved pew. We won't have to search for a place to sit." Martha straightened her hat and took her son's arm.

"That pew cost me a bundle." Lester opened Sara's door, and offered her his arm. The two couples made their way across the street, with Martha complaining every step of the way about them jaywalking.

One of Grandma's sage sayings slid through Sara mind. *Some folks wouldn't be satisfied if they had the world with a fence around it. They'd grumble because there wasn't a pearl in every post.*

Chapter Fourteen

June 25, 1945
Monday Morning

Sara woke early to see Kent picking up his brief case. She had some questions for him. "Don't go just yet. I have some things I want to ask you."

"Make it quick. Father is probably waiting for me." He laid his briefcase in a chair, came across the room, and sat on the bed beside her. "I'm listening."

"I want to know why you never came into the church service yesterday morning." Sara swung her feet to the floor. "Where did you go and why?"

"Didn't Father explain? He asked me to go to the dealership to attend to some urgent business." He stood, walked across the floor, and picked up his briefcase. "I really should be on my way." At the door, he threw her a kiss and then closed it behind him.

Sara sat on the side of the bed. Lester's explanation had all the trappings of a lie. Kent's account wasn't much better. This man was her husband. She should trust him.

She put the matter from her mind and thought of what she would do to occupy her time today. She had read all the books she'd checked out from the library. She could walk to the branch library. Too hot, she decided. She needed something useful to occupy her time.

She bathed, dressed, and went downstairs, still rotating in her mind ways she could spend her day.

When she entered the kitchen, Mrs. Mac turned from the stove to look at her in surprise. "What are you doing up at this hour?"

"Looking for a cup of coffee."

"Grab a mug." Mrs. Mac pointed toward the cabinet. "Coffee's on the stove. Would you like some breakfast?"

"Dry cereal will do." Sara poured steaming coffee into a mug.

"I have scrambled eggs and Spam left over from the breakfast I made for the two Mr. Holdens. There's plenty for both of us." Mrs. Mac waved her spatula. "Sit down." She carried two plates filled with Spam, eggs, and toast toward the table. The food smelled heavenly.

Where is Izzie?" Sara looked around the kitchen.

"Huh," Mrs. Mac harrumphed. "She's not here yet. That girl gets to work when she gets ready, and ready is usually around ten o'clock." She put one plate in front of Sara and another in front of the chair across the table before she sat down. "I ask God to bless the food I eat." She bowed her head, said a short blessing, and then looked up. "Dive in."

Sara ate heartily. The food was delicious. "I will have to do this more often."

"Don't let her Highness catch you." Mrs. Mac pointed her fork in Sara's direction. "She would pitch a royal fit if she found her son's wife eating in the kitchen with the hired help."

"Do you really think so?" Sara asked, surprise lifting her voice.

"I know so. Queen Martha has delusions of grandeur."

"Don't let her catch you saying such things about her." Sara once again looked around the room. "She will fire you, for sure."

"She won't fire me." Mrs. Mac took a sip of coffee. "Mr. Holden wouldn't let her. If he did, I could get another job in a New York minute."

"I don't know." Sara frowned. "That woman has a way of getting what she wants, even though Lester is less than kind to her at times."

"They're the strangest couple I ever met. I've been working here almost eighteen months and I haven't figured out the two of them yet. Want some jam? It's blackberry, homemade. I put it up myself."

"Yes, I would."

Mrs. Mac went to the pantry, returned with the jam, opened it, and set it on the table. Sara spread a liberal amount over a slice of toast. "I will miss your cooking when Kent and I move into a place of our own."

"When will you be leaving?" Mrs. Mac took a sip of coffee.

"Not for a while," Sara said. "Houses to rent are scarce as hen's teeth."

"I know about a house for rent." Mrs. Mac spread jam over her remaining slice of toast. "The people who own it are particular about who they rent to, but you and Mr. Holden just might be acceptable tenants."

"A house?" Sara laid her fork across her plate. "Really? Tell me about it."

"Okay, and if I don't get canned for this, I have a job for life." Mrs. Mac smiled and leaned across the table.

*****

Sara got off the bus and studied the neighborhood around her. It was a far cry from the Holdens' community. Everything from the unpaved roads to the small, shabby, older houses, shouted underprivileged. Despite its poor circumstance, there was an air of congeniality about the place. Patrons waved and chatted as they came and went into a mom-and-pop grocery store across the way. Children played in front yards. Teenagers rode bicycles up and down the bumpy street.

Sara sat on the bus bench and once again read the letter of instructions Mrs. Mac wrote for her.

Get off the bus at the corner of Pine Avenue and Ardmore Street. Turn right on Ardmore and go two blocks. In the third block, the third house on the right is where Agnes lives. Give her this note and tell her I sent you. She will show you the house.

Sara walked down Ardmore Street. It was a pleasant journey. Gardens flourished in back yards. Freshly washed clothes flapped on clothes lines. Flowers bloomed in neatly-kept beds. She was in the third block and counting houses before it occurred to her that the only name she knew for the person she was seeking was Agnes.

Agnes, here I come. She went up the walk and across the porch to the front door, knocked, and crossed her fingers.

The young woman who answered the door was skinny and at least six feet tall. Her wealth of brown hair was pulled back into a knot at the nape of her neck. She stared down at Sara with a questioning expression on her gaunt countenance. "Yes, can I help you?"

"Mrs. MacNay sent me," Sara blurted out. "It's about the house you have for rent. She gave me a note to give to you." She opened her purse. "I have it right here."

"You know Tessie?" The woman unhooked the screen and opened it. "Let me see that note."

Sara put the note into a long, lean hand.

The woman re-hooked the screen before looking at the message. As she read, a smile spread across her angular face. "Yep, that's Tessie's handwriting all right." She once more unhooked the screen, and pushed it open. "Come in, and we can talk."

Sara stepped from outside and into a neatly-kept living room.

The woman waved one hand. "Find a place and sit down."

Sara perched on the end of a worn couch. "My name is Sara Holden. My husband and I are interested in the house you have for rent." At least Sara was interested. Kent would be interested when she told him about it.

"My name is Agnes Balcombe." The woman sat across from her in a wooden rocker. "Tell me how you came to know Tessie."

"Mrs. MacNay is my mother-in-law's cook."

"That's not much of a recommendation," Agnes announced bluntly. "Still, if Tessie vouches for you, you must be okay. Before we go to see the house there are some things you should know and some questions I have to ask."

"Like what?" Why was she being so mysterious?

"The house is a parsonage. It's behind the Grace Bible Church."

"Why would you want to rent your parsonage?"

Agnes frowned as she said, "Our pastor bought a house across the street from the church. He has a wife and five kids. Seven people won't fit into that little parsonage."

"Why don't you sell it?" Sara asked.

"It would be nice if we could." Agnes's lips drew into a thin line. "Pastor Timothy, the pastor we had before we called Pastor Frank, built the parsonage. He borrowed the money to build the house by mortgaging the church. He connected the house's utilities to the church's utilities. The church and the house are on the same loan. That's why if we sell the house, we have to sell the church along with it." She eyed Sara cautiously. "Are you still interested in seeing it?"

"I am indeed." Sara couldn't imagine why the house hadn't already been rented. "Does it have a yard?"

""It has a fenced yard. It's unfurnished, has two bedrooms and a bath, and rents for twelve dollars a month. Of course, the utilities are included."

""Can I see it now?" Sara stood and hooked her purse over her arm.

"There are a few other things we have to discuss." Agnes didn't move. "Sit down." Sara sat, wondering as she did so, what else there could be left *to* discuss.

Out of the blue Agnes asked, "Do you smoke?"

"No." Sara laid her purse beside her on the couch. "Why do you ask?"

"The parsonage is behind our church. The deacons all agree that it wouldn't be proper for someone living there who smokes."

"My husband smokes a pipe." *I knew this was too good to be true.*

"Men don't count," Agnes said, with a wave of one hand. "If they did, the Good Lord knows we'd be shy a couple of deacons."

"Is there anything else?" Sara bit her lip to keep from smiling.

"Just one other thing," Agnes said. "You will not be home during Sunday morning church services. You can come to our church. We'd be glad to have you. If that's not to your liking, you can go to another church, or visit friends, or go to a movie. Just so long as you aren't in the parsonage during that time. To have our renters at home while we are having Sunday morning services wouldn't speak well for our church."

Sara was poised to tell Agnes that she was no longer interested in the house. Then she remembered the other places she'd seen, and how long she would wait before she could move into one of them. During that time, she would be living with Martha and Lester. "May I see the house now?"

Chapter Fifteen

June 25, 1945
Monday Night

"I found a house we can rent," Sara announced with delight, the moment she and Kent were alone in their sitting room.

"When did this miracle occur? Where is it?" Kent sat in an easy chair and tamped tobacco into his pipe. "I'm surprised Pete didn't call me."

"Pete didn't find this house. Mrs. Mac told me about it. I paid our first month's rent. It's unfurnished. We will have to buy furniture." Sara's words tumbled over each other in their haste to be said. "It has two bedrooms and a fenced yard. It's small, but adequate for the two of us. It rents for only twelve dollars a month, and the utilities are paid. We can—"

"Whoa." Kent held up one hand. "Where is this house?"

"It's on the east side, on Ada Street. I have such plans. I can plant a fall garden. We can—"

"That's a rather unsavory section of town." Kent laid his pipe aside and frowned. "I can't believe you rented a house before I saw it and we talked about it."

"I thought you'd be happy that I found a place for us." His response was not what Sara expected. "The neighborhood is not upscale, neither is it unsavory. The houses are clean and the yards well-kept." After a long moment of silence, she added, "I thought you would be pleased."

"I'm trying to be. I think you acted rather hastily." Kent picked up his pipe and lit it. "What's done is done."

"I couldn't take the chance of letting this opportunity slip by." Sara's joy deflated like a punctured balloon.

"Who owns the house?" Kent's eyes narrowed. "What is his name? I would like to speak with him."

"What makes you assume the house belongs to a man?" Annoyance itched down Sara's spine.

"Tell me *her* name."

Sara's irritation overrode her common sense. "The house belongs to the Grace Bible Church. It's behind their building. It was once their parsonage."

"You rented a house that's behind a church?" Kent catapulted to his feet.

"Had you rather live behind a bar?" Sara snapped, before she could rein in her anger. Maybe she had acted hastily. In a much gentler voice, she asked, "Will you at least look at it before you decide it's unsuitable?"

"It's not necessary. If it pleases you, I will make the best of the situation." The lines around Kent's mouth deepened. His eyes always spoke his emotion. They clouded as if he were in pain. He moved toward the bedroom. "Good night. I had a difficult day. I need some rest."

"No. Wait," Sara called after him.

His answer was to disappear into the bedroom.

Sara curled up on the end of the couch and wished for something to read. As large and impressive as this house was, she had yet to find one book anywhere in it. There were rooms and to spare, but no library, not even a bookcase tucked away in some out-of-the-way alcove.

Loneliness, like a shroud, fell around her shoulders. Was it possible to love her husband even though she didn't know him? She was beginning to realize what a complex man Kent was. Just when she thought she understood him, he reacted in a way she could not comprehend.

If she went to bed now, with her heart aching, and her mind teeming with polarizing thoughts, she wouldn't sleep. She had no desire to lie for hours beside Kent in a wide-awake state.

I do have something to read. She went to the entrance way closet and dug around in her half-unpacked suitcase until she found her Bible.

When she had once again settled on the couch, she opened the book, kicked off her shoes, tucked her feet under her, and read:

> *By reason of the voice of my groaning, my bones cleave to my skin.*
> *I am like a pelican in the wilderness. I am like an owl in the desert.*
> *I watch, and am as a sparrow alone upon the house top. Psalm 102:5-7 KJV*

The words brought little comfort. She was like that poor little sparrow. Alone in an unfamiliar world. It had been a long time since Sara prayed, really prayed, instead of mouthing words from a sense of duty. "Lord, please help me. Protect and guide your little sparrow."

Brawling voices from downstairs blasted up the stairway and echoed down the hall. The words were indistinct. The tones were explosive. Sara hurried to the stairs, and leaned over the banister.

Kent tied the belt of his bathrobe as he came to stand behind her. "What is going on down there?"

Lester came up the stairs to the second-floor landing and skidded to a halt. "Mother is having a conniption fit. She fired Mrs. Mac. Come and help me calm her down." He turned and rushed back down the stairs, taking two steps at a time.

'What am I supposed to do?" Kent asked as he followed Lester down the stairs. For a few indecisive moments, Sara stood at the head of the stairs. Martha's voice pierced her eardrums. "How could you stoop so low as to stab me in the back? I say again, you're fired."

You can't fire me, *Queen* Martha!" Mrs. Mac's echoing response split the air. "I quit."

"Oh, no." Sara rushed down the steps and toward the sound of loud voices.

Chapter Sixteen

June 27, 1945
Wednesday Morning

Sara stirred when Kent got out of the bed and slipped his feet into his house slippers. He sat on the side of the bed and let his head fall into his hands.
"Kent?" she questioned.
"Go back to sleep." He stood and moved toward the bathroom.
Sara got out of bed. There would be time enough to sleep later, after she and Kent settled their differences. Events from Monday evening played through her head like a clip from a bad movie.
She had arrived downstairs to see Mrs. Mac facing Martha with both hands on her hips. "You have no business butting into my personal affairs."
Lester stood on the sidelines, shaking his head and muttering under his breath.
"Quiet down, both of you." Kent stepped between the two angry women. "We can settle this problem peacefully." He looked toward Lester. "What *is* the problem?"
Izzie huddled in a chair in a far corner. "I didn't do anything wrong."
"You stay out of this." Mrs. Mac shook her fist in Izzie's direction, making the frightened girl scrunch farther down in her chair.
Sara put a forefinger in each corner of her mouth and let go with a long, keen whistle. Sudden silence fell over the room as five sets of wary eyes stared in her direction. She extended one hand toward the dining room table. "Sit down, everybody." She added a profound "Please."
One-by-one each person took a place at the table; Lester first, then Kent. Next came Martha, and then Mrs. Mac. Izzie scooted her chair between Lester and Kent, as if she would assure her protection by sitting between two big men.
What do I do now? Sara asked herself as she sat in the one remaining vacant chair.
Much to her surprise, and to her relief, Kent took charge.

*****

"Sara. Hello, Sarah?" Someone calling her name pulled Sara back from her wandering thoughts. She shook her head as the past faded into the present. Kent stared down at her. "We do need to talk." He was dressed for work and had his briefcase under his arm. He bent and kissed her on the cheek. "I will try to come home early tonight."

"No." Sara caught his sleeve. "You have spent an entire day dodging this issue. Tonight is too far away. We need to talk now."

"What is there to say that can't wait?" Kent sighed as he sat in a chair and laid his briefcase on the antique table beside it. "Mother apologized to Mrs. Mac for firing her and asked her to stay on as cook. Father gave her a twenty-dollar-a-month raise. Izzie apologized to you and Mrs. Mac for eavesdropping on your conversation about the house and blabbing to Mother about it. The entire episode was a tempest in a tea pot."

Kent might believe the matter was settled, but Sara didn't, not for one minute. At this moment the little occurrence Monday night was not what was uppermost in her mind. "There is something else we have to settle. It's about the house I rented. Why are you so dead set against living there?"

"I don't like being so close to a church." Kent stood and took his billfold from his pocket. "Buy the furniture you need." He took out several large denomination bills and laid them on the little table. "Try to be patient with Mother today." He put his billfold in his pocket, once more tucked his briefcase under his arm, and turned toward the door.

"Wait." Sara hurried to him and pulled him around to face her. She put her arms around his waist. "I love you. I'm trying very hard to adjust to my new surroundings. Be patient with me."

Kent's briefcase hit the floor with a plop. He drew her into his arms and kissed her passionately.

She responded with ardent fervor.

He released her and stared down into her eyes. "Everything is going to be all right. Buy your furniture. Be happy. I love you." He picked up his briefcase and left.

It would be all right. Just as soon as they got out of this crazy house. Sara sat in the chair Kent had vacated. It had to be. She loved this man too much to ever let him go.

A harassing little voice in the back of her head whispered, *You love a stranger? Are you sure?*

Sara tried to ignore its nagging. It persisted, like the haunting refrain of some old, half-forgotten melody.

June 29, 1945
Friday Morning

Sara looked around the room. *My kitchen.* She had found a gas cook stove that was apartment size. At twenty-one inches wide and twenty-nine inches deep, it fit nicely in one corner of the kitchen. She might have to learn to cook all over again. Her experience had always been with a wood stove.

Her Frigidaire refrigerator rested snugly beside the cabinet. It was a real refrigerator with a place to make ice cubes. On the farm they didn't even have an ice box. Ice hauled from Cedar Gap to home was wrapped in a quilt and left in the shade on the front porch.

The kitchen was perfect. She loved it. Once more, Sara looked around the room. A drop-leaf table and four chairs stood beneath a window. When it wasn't in use, she could drop both leaves and slide it against the wall, giving more space to navigate from cabinet to stove. She would soon make curtains for the windows, with matching cushions for the kitchen chairs.

She went into the living room. A wicker sofa and two matching chairs were arranged around the room. She suspected the set was patio furniture. It was too bold, with its lime green color and orange and white striped cushions. Nevertheless, Sara knew a bargain when she saw one. If she covered those cushions with a solid muted color, and painted the wicker a warm shade of brown, she would have a nice set of living room furniture.

Identical end tables stood at each arm of the couch. One of the wicker chairs was a rocker.

Her one extravagance was a large, comfortable easy chair for Kent.

Her heart overflowed with joy as she traveled to the front bedroom. She had found a beautiful art deco bedroom set, complete with a waterfall dresser and chest. On the farm she slept on an iron bedstead that was a gift from Grandma, who laughed and said it came over on the Mayflower.

The back bedroom was vacant of furniture, except for the treadle sewing machine she bought. Maybe she shouldn't have, but it was such a bargain. When Kent had time, they would go to the farm and get the remainder of her belongings, including her bed and chest of drawers, and the cedar chest that was her high school graduation gift from Mama and Daddy. She could use the back bedroom for her sewing. She had so many things to make and so many things to do.

She gathered the tools she brought to work with, put them in a shopping bag, hung her purse over her shoulder and stepped outside. She planned, as she walked to the bus stop, all the things she would do to make her house a home. What was a home without children? The thought came swiftly and stabbed deeply. *I will change his mind. I will. I will.*

Chapter Seventeen

June 29, 1945
Friday Evening

Sara was weary by the time she reached Kent's parents' home. She had missed a city bus connection and was forced to stand in the heat an extra half-hour.

Martha met her at the door. "You are late. It's almost dinner time. Kent and Lester will be home soon."

Her plans to move into the house she had rented was a sore subject between Sara and her mother-in-law. She would not tell Martha that the house was ready for occupancy. That meant not mentioning to Kent all she wanted to tell him until they were alone.

"I'm sorry." Sara didn't recall telling Martha when she would be home. She could have informed the overbearing woman of that fact. What would be the point? "I missed a bus connection."

"Don't dilly dally. Get inside and get ready for dinner." Martha opened the door wide and motioned with one hand. "You know how I dislike anyone being late for meals."

It took all of Sara's willpower to hold onto her temper and her tongue. She found comfort in the knowledge that this time next week, she and Kent would be in their own home. She made for the stairs as swiftly as possible. She didn't stop her rapid pace until she was standing in front of her own quarters.

She had scarcely washed her face and hands and combed her hair when Izzie knocked on the door. "Miz. Holden says come downstairs. Mr. Holden and your husband are washing up for supper. I mean dinner."

"I'm coming," Sara replied. She couldn't get out of this place fast enough.

She entered the dining room to see Martha wringing her hands as she waited. Kent and Lester were nowhere in sight. She immediately took Sara to task. "It is seven minutes after seven. When are the residents of this house going to realize that dinner is served promptly at seven o'clock?"

"Not tonight." Kent came from behind and put his arms around Sara's waist. He kissed her cheek. "Did you have a good day?"

"I did," Sara replied, and then asked, "Did you?"

"He sold three used cars." Lester appeared at her side. "Yes siree. That son of mine is quite a salesman. He—"

"Lester, you are late for dinner." Martha pointed to a chair. "Sit down, all of you. It's fifteen minutes past seven." She pressed her hand across her forehead and massaged her temples. "Why is my life so difficult?"

The three offenders hurried to be seated around the table.

Sara wanted to say so many things. She kept her mouth shut. Soon she and Kent would be out of this house and snug in their own home.

She ate her meal in silence as she listened to Lester extol Kent's exceptional abilities as a salesman.

Martha waved her fork in his direction. "Can you talk about something else? You are boring me to tears."

Lester, who usually did his wife's bidding, took immediate offense. "Don't tell me what I can talk about at my supper table. If I want to brag on Kent, I will."

"You are uncouth and impossible." Martha's voice rose in pitch and volume. "How often have I told you the evening meal is called *dinner*?"

"I clean forgot. All right, dinner and I'm gonna talk about what I please. So there."

"Mrs. Mac made a cake using honey," Martha said, in a much milder tone. "She says that will help us conserve sugar."

"That sounds mighty fine to me." Lester spoke between shoveling big bites of a Spam casserole into his mouth. "Tell Izzie to bring it on."

Sara sent Kent a questioning look.

He smiled and shrugged.

The meal was completed without further differences between Lester and Martha.

Sara didn't relax until she and Kent were inside their sitting room. "I thought your mother would object to us leaving so soon after dinner was over."

"You must learn not to pay heed to anything Mother says or doesn't say." Kent took off his tie and draped it over the arm of a chair. "She is a childish, domineering woman."

"That's a cruel thing to say." Sara was shocked by his harsh assessment of the woman who had cared for and nurtured him since his early childhood.

"Sara, Sara. When will you learn?" He sat on the settee and stretched his legs out in front of him. "Sometimes the truth *is* cruel."

Sara dismissed his words with a wave of one hand. "I have so many things to tell you. Our house is ready. We can move in Monday." She sat beside him and took his hands in hers. "Do you have a pickup at the car lot that we can use? I have furniture and other things at the farm. When can we go for them? Tomorrow we can go to see our new home. On Monday we can move in—"

"Slow down." Kent pulled his hands free. "Let's take these things one at a time. In two days, you have that house furnished and ready to move into? How did you manage that?"

"I bought the furniture and hired a transfer company to deliver it. The appliance store where I bought the cook stove and refrigerator delivered them and connected the stove for me. They charged extra, but not much. I—"

Kent interrupted again, "You did all that with the money I gave you?"

"I can return the sewing machine." Was he angry or surprised? She didn't know. "I had six dollars and fifty-seven cents left. Do you want that back?"

"What I want is for you to tell me what you bought and where you bought it." He leaned forward and narrowed his eyes.

"I bought several things and I shopped several places." He was behaving as if she had done something wrong. "They were all bargains. The table and chairs need painting. I can do that. I'm going to recover and paint the couch and chairs."

"You bought second hand furniture?" Kent stood, and stared down at her. "Why?"

"Sit down, please." He was making her uneasy, standing above her, staring down with that frown on his face. "I knew what we needed. I knew how much money I had. I shopped accordingly." It had never occurred her to do otherwise.

"I thought you would buy one or two new items. I never dreamed you would go to a second-hand store."

"You told me to get what I needed." She had disappointed him when she thought he would be proud of her. Tears formed in her eyes.

He sat down and put his arms around her. "Don't cry. It was just a misunderstanding. It doesn't matter."

It did matter and Sara knew it did. A chill collected around her heart. They were worlds apart on so many issues that were important to both of them. She grew up knowing the worth of a dollar and being taught to be thrifty and always to look for bargains.

"It's all right. We will work it out." He kissed her gently.

Maybe if he saw the house? "Tomorrow when you see all the things I got, you will feel better about everything."

"I can't go tomorrow." He lifted her chin and looked into her eyes. "It's our busiest day at the dealership. We will go Sunday morning."

They couldn't go Sunday morning either. Sara refrained from saying so. She moved closer to him.

He kissed her passionately.

She responded with fire and fervor as she surrendered to his magical touch. Whatever was amiss could be fixed because they loved each other.

Later, as she lay beside her sleeping husband, relaxed and staring at the ceiling, Sara's mind replayed their earlier conversation. That nagging little voice that had plagued her so often lately, whispered inside her head. *You lied to your husband.*

I did not. I would never lie to Kent.

Sometimes silence is a lie.

Sara fell into a troubled sleep, still arguing with herself.

Chapter Eighteen

July 1, 1945
Sunday

Martha insisted Sara and Kent attend Sunday morning services, and that Kent wear his uniform and his medals. "I want my friends to see what a hero my son is."

"Sara and I have other plans—" Kent began.

"This is important to Mother." Lester bulldozed his way into the conversation. "She's proud of you, son. So am I." He turned toward Sara. "Tell him, girl, how important it is to attend church on Sunday morning."

Sara was set to attempt Kent's rescue when she recalled she had yet to tell him why they couldn't visit their house until afternoon. "It's important to attend church, period." *I am a coward.*

"Let's get the show on the road." Lester rubbed his hands together.

"Are you okay with going to the house after lunch?" Kent asked Sara.

Sara nodded her consent. She was only postponing the inevitable. She had to tell Kent about not being home on Sunday mornings, and she had to tell him soon.

"Okay, I'll go, and I'll wear my uniform, and all my medals."

Their Sunday morning was a replay of the Sunday morning before. Martha and Lester traded insults and snapped at each other as they drove downtown. Once there, they argued over where to park.

They finally made it into the church. It was dim and cool inside. An usher showed them to their pew.

Just after the opening prayer, Kent left her side, and then the sanctuary.

Sara stood to follow him.

Lester caught her arm and pulled her back down into the pew. "Let him be, girl. He won't go far."

She sat back down. People in the pews around them were staring at her. She lowered her head and wished she had the nerve to follow Kent.

The services were cold and formal. Sara had trouble staying awake. Finally, the last song was sung and the last amen uttered.

The crowd moved slowly up the aisle. As they reached the vestibule, she spied Kent waiting for them just inside the entrance.

Martha took her son's arm. "There you are. Come along. I want you to meet some of my friends." She lingered, long after services, introducing Kent to everyone she could capture and bragging about his brave feats as a war hero.

Lester stood just outside the entrance, chewing on the end of an unlit cigar, and smiling from ear to ear. Sara stood beside him, feeling small and unnecessary.

The last few parishioners were wandering away before Martha and Kent said goodbye to the weary-faced pastor and made their exit.

Lester took them to lunch at a cafeteria with beautiful surroundings and a wide array of food.

Sara's appetite waned when she thought that she had yet to tell Kent of her promise not to be in their house on Sunday mornings. Her uncertainty about how he would react aggravated her anxiety over not having told him sooner. She had always prided herself on her honesty and her straightforward manner. She justified her behavior by telling herself she had never been so uncertain before. Deep in her heart, she knew that was an excuse, not a reason.

The moment Lester pulled into the driveway of his house, he stopped the car and gave Kent the keys. "Get out, Martha. These young people have places to go."

"Not before I get out of this uniform and into some cooler clothes." Kent got out of the car and opened the back car door for his mother.

"Fool's errand." Martha turned and slid until her feet touched the ground. "'What kind of idiots would even consider living behind a church?"

"Now, Mother, this is not your business." Lester opened the back door for Sara.

"You are all right with Kent leaving home." Martha was midway to the front door. She stopped and faced her husband. "You will continue to see him every day at work. Once he's from under our roof, who knows when I will see him again? I will never be a part of his life again." She spun around and made hurried steps toward the door. "Why is my life so hard?"

"Pay no heed to Mother." Lester helped Sara from the car. "That's just her way."

Someone should bring her to account for what she says and does. Sara took Lester's arm and let him escort her toward the door. One of these days she just might get around to being that someone.

Once they were upstairs, Kent took off his uniform. "I am glad to get out of that hot suit. It's like being in a steam bath." He put on cool cotton pants and a light tee shirt. The muscles in his arms rippled. His pants accentuated his slim waist and narrow hips.

"Sit down, please." Sara could no longer deceive the man she loved. "I have something to tell you."

"You sound serious." Kent sat. "I hope it's not bad news."

Sara took a deep breath. There was no tactful way to deliver disquieting news. "We can't be at home when the church in front of us is having services on Sunday mornings." There, she had said it. She closed her eyes and waited for his response.

"That's good news. I was afraid they might insist on us coming to their meetings."

His words rang in her ears and echoed through her head.

"You don't mind?" She opened her eyes.

"I'm relieved." He stood. "That takes us off the hook for attending church, period. Are you ready to go see our house?"

"You don't *want* to go to church?" Once again, his words surprised her. They also disturbed her. "Why?"

"Let it go, Sara." His expression darkened.

"I can't let it go. Attending church is an important part of my life." A terrifying thought took her. "Don't you believe in God?"

"I believe in you and me." He caught her hands and pulled her to her feet. "Let's go to our new home. I'm anxious to see where you and I will start our lives together."

Sara took his arm. It will work out, she assured herself. But her misgivings lingered like an unwanted guest. The couple made their way downstairs and into the car.

She was tempted, as they drove across the city, to once more bring up the subject of church. Instead, she kept her conversation light.

Kent was non-committal until she mentioned going to the farm. "It may be a few weeks before we can make the trip." He glanced briefly in her direction before looking back at the road.

It was not so much what he said as the dismissive way he said it, that sent sparks of anger singing through Sara. "You don't have to go with me. I can make the trip alone. All I need is a pickup." She stiffened her backbone and waited for his cutting reply.

"*Can* you manage alone?" She heard no anger and only a touch of surprise. "It would be a help if you could. Father has given me complete charge of the used car department of the business. I need to be there every day."

'I can manage." She hid her anger behind a benign smile. "I will leave as soon as I have transportation." Was his job more important than getting moved into their home? Obviously, that was the case.

"How much farther?" Kent slowed for a stop sign.

"Turn left at the next red light."

Chapter Nineteen

July 4, 1945
Wednesday Morning

Sara came down the stairs with her suitcase in one hand and her purse slung over her shoulder. She was anxious about making the trip to Cedar Gap alone, but her pride refused to let her admit that. She had thought Kent would change his mind and go with her when he realized she intended to make the trip alone if he didn't. He hadn't. She thought of James refusing to let her drive alone from the farm to Cedar Gap. Her hurt ran deep. Her pride ran deeper. *I can do this alone. I don't need Kent.*

She came into the foyer to see Martha and Izzie waiting for her. Izzie had a well-worn suitcase by her side.

"Izzie is going with you," Martha announced before Sara could speak. "It's not proper for my daughter-in-law to go chasing across the country alone. What will people think? What will they say?"

"Don't you need Izzie here?" Sara sat her suitcase on the floor. Was everyone in this house crazy? She was beginning to think so. "I may be gone three or four days."

"Izzie won't be missed. She does very little around here anyway."

"In that case, why do you keep her?" The words hopped over Sara's better judgment and out of her mouth before she could stop them.

"A woman in my position should have a maid." Martha folded her arms across her chest as if that settled the matter.

Sara was too happy to have a companion along to argue. "Okay, Izzie, let's go." She picked up her suitcase and then sat it back down. "You do want to go with me, don't you?"

"Oh, yes ma'am, Miss Sara. I truly want to go."

"Forget the Miss. My name is Sara." Once more Sara got a firm grip on her suitcase. "Let's get the show on the road." She exited the foyer with Izzie, suitcase in hand, following close behind her.

They were scarcely inside the pickup before Izzie began to ask questions. "How far is it to Cedar Gap? How long will it take us to get there? Have you ever driven a pickup before?"

"Slow down. One question at a time." Sara pulled from the driveway and onto the street. "The trip should take somewhere in the neighborhood of three-and-a-half to four hours. It's around one hundred and fifty miles."

"I have never been out of Houston before." Izzie touched the knob on the gear shift. "How do you know when to shift this thing around?"

"It's something that after you learn, it takes time and practice to do well." Sara explained the details of shifting gears and how the clutch played an important role. Izzie listened carefully and then asked Sara to explain again.

They passed the city limits sign of Houston. The road stretched ahead like an unwinding ribbon. Traffic thinned. Sara relaxed and settled down for a long ride. Her thoughts strayed to recent past events. Kent could at least have been there to tell her goodbye. Did he think she wouldn't go without him? He was wrong, so wrong. "Miss Sara, can we eat dinner, I mean lunch, in a café?" Izzie's question impinged on Sara's wandering thoughts.

"Call me Sara, *please*. I don't know, maybe."

"Mrs. Holden said we couldn't. She made Mrs. Mac pack us a lunch."

"She did, did she?" Sara wasn't surprised. She was spitting mad.

"Yes, ma'am. I have it in my suitcase."

"You can leave it there. We will eat in a café." Sara reined in her anger and concentrated on driving. How dare Martha try to tell her where she could and couldn't eat?

"Can I have a hamburger and fried potatoes?"

"Most definitely."

"How fast are you driving?" Izzie leaned toward Sara and looked at the speedometer. "What are all those other gadgets for?"

"I'm driving fifty miles per hour. One of those gadgets tells me how fast I'm driving. Another shows how much gasoline is in the gas tank." Her questions were beginning to annoy Sara. "Don't worry about the other gadgets."

"I'm not worried, I like to find out things. You could drive sixty miles an hour. That's the speed limit in the daytime."

"What's the speed limit at night?" Sara asked. She was surprised Izzie was aware of the daytime speed limit.

"Night time is fifty-five miles an hour."

"Who told you that?"

"I listen when people talk. You might be surprised at what some of them say when they think no one is listening."

"That's eavesdropping." Sara stared briefly in the girl's direction. The sly look in her eyes was fleeting and unsettling. She shifted her gaze back to the road.

July 4, 1945
Wednesday Noon

Long before Sara reached the top of the hill that led to the little town of Cactus Gulley, strains of music impinged on her ears.

"Somebody's having a party." Izzie stuck her head out the pickup window. The wind blew in her face, distorting her features, and sending her hair flying in all directions. She drew her head back inside. "Can we go, Sara, please?"

"We weren't invited." Sara topped the hill. Far down the slope, a marching band and several riders on horseback came into view. "It's a parade."

The band and riders rounded a corner. Several floats followed. Martial music blasted the air. Flags flew from the sides of each float. Like a punch in the mid-section, the thought registered. *It's the Fourth of July.*

"Can we eat in a café now?" Izzie ran her fingers through her hair. 'I'm really hungry."

"Yes." Sara turned south onto a side road. She too felt the pangs produced by an empty stomach. "We will have to circle the main part of town in order to get around the parade." She turned onto the first road that headed west. The street was deserted. "Everyone must be at the parade."

"Can we stop and watch the parade?" Izzie clapped her hands together. "Please?"

"No."

"Why?"

Why indeed? This was a national holiday and Sara was alone in a little one-horse town halfway between her husband and her family. Not quite alone. She had Izzie. "Yes." She slowed and turned north.

After she found a parking spot near the center of town, She and Izzie and walked the two blocks to the street where the parade was marching.

"Hurry, Sara." Izzie sped ahead. "If we walk fast, we will see all of the parade."

Sara quickened her step to keep pace with the excited girl.

"I have never seen anything like this before." Izzie grabbed Sara's hand and pushed through crowd. The group lining the street responded with hateful looks and disparaging complaints.

Izzie ignored them and shoved through until they stood on the front row of spectators.

The parade was a typical small-town procession, with the high school band, the mayor and council members riding in classic automobiles, trail riders on horse-back, the high school drill team wearing short skirts and stepping high, and Veterans from World War One shuffling along, out of step. Some of them had managed to squeeze into their old uniforms.

Elaborately decorated floats representing area businesses and organizations brought up the rear. The last float carried Miss Cactus Gulley. Sara smiled and shook her head. Who in their right mind would want to be crowned Miss Cactus Gulley?

Despite her criticism, she was caught up in the excitement that permeated the air.

As the last float rounded a corner and disappeared from view, Sara turned to the plump little elderly woman standing beside her. "Can you direct us to a nearby restaurant?"

"Heavenly days, girl." The woman stared over the granny glasses that perched on the end of her nose. "Every business in Cactus Gulley is closed today. Everybody in ten square miles of town is headed to the city park. You're invited if you'd like to come along."

"We *are* invited." Izzie clapped her hands. "Where is the park?"

"That way." The woman pointed in a westerly direction. "Just follow the crowd."
.

Chapter Twenty

July 4, 1945
Wednesday Afternoon

The park with its green lawn and many shade trees was situated between a firehouse on the north and a river on the south. Narrow streets marked its east and west boundaries. A domed pavilion stood near the river bank in a grove of live oak trees. A high chain link fence behind it denied access to the peaceful waterway. Three picnic tables were pushed together. They groaned beneath a heavy load of barbeque, potato salad, pinto beans, cole slaw, rolls, pecan pies, and jugs of iced tea.

"Welcome to our annual Fourth of July celebration." A tall, rangy, balding man stood at the head of the tables. "This annual affair is sponsored by the merchants, business men, and civic-minded citizens of Cactus Gulch. We are celebrating the birthday of our country. What a glorious history—"

A deep voice from the crowd called out, "Get on with blessing the food, pastor. You can preach us a sermon next Sunday morning."

Murmurs of approval from the group echoed his request, or was it a demand?

The tall man raised his hand, bowed his head, and asked God to bless an array of people and things. He ended his appeal by asking blessings on "this splendid display of food."

Sara and Izzie filled their plates and sat on the ground under the shade of a cottonwood tree. The food was delicious. Midway through their meal, the chubby woman with the granny glasses approached them. "May I keep you company?"

"We would be glad for your company." Sara patted the space beside her. "Please, sit down."

"Do you think she should?" Izzie jumped to her feet. "She's old. What if she can't get up?"

"Don't be silly, child." The woman sat beside Sara. "I'm spry as a spring chicken." She sat and put her plate down beside her. "My name is Abigail Morgan. You can call me Abbie."

"Yes, ma'am." Izzie sat again and picked up her plate.

Sara introduced herself and Izzie, explained their mission, and how they arrived in Cactus Gully just in time to see the parade.

'It was a good parade," Izzie said. "The dinner is good too." She slapped her hand over her mouth and pulled it away. "Oops, I meant to say lunch."

"It's all right, Izzie." Sara addressed Abigail. "We have enjoyed your celebration." A baseball from a group of teenagers' baseball game hit the ground and rolled to Sara. She tossed it to the advancing left fielder. He caught it in his glove, tipped his cap, and trotted back to the game.

"Thank you for inviting us." Izzie wiped her face with a paper napkin. "I don't know when I've had such good fun."

"We haven't even begun to celebrate." Abigail pointed toward the pavilion. "In a few minutes The Muddy Bottom River Boys Band will be here to play. Some of the people will be dancing. I don't hold with dancing myself, but to each his own, I always say. After dark, there will be a fireworks display. That's my kind of entertainment. You're invited to stay, if you'd like."

"I would like," Izzie said, and then bit into her slice of pecan pie.

"So would I," Sara agreed. "But we can't. We should be on the road if we want to get to the farm before dark."

"You can go there tomorrow." Abbie went on to explain. "You can stay at the church tonight. We have rooms and beds and a nice bathroom and kitchen. It's the place where pastors and their families stay when we have our annual fall revival and missionary conference."

"Can we?" Izzie begged. "Please, Sara, can we?"

"I don't think so." Sara frowned. "We can't just appear at a church and expect to stay there overnight." The preacher who led the prayer at noon didn't strike her as the most approachable man she'd ever met. What if he were the pastor of Abbie's church? "What would the pastor think? What would he say?"

"The pastor is my husband," Abbie declared, with a great amount of indignation. "He will think what I tell him to think. He will say what I tell him to say. Come on, girls, let's go listen to the music."

This was the most outrageous thing she had ever done. Nevertheless, Sara followed Abbie and Izzie toward the bandstand, censuring herself with every step she took.

July 5, 1945
Thursday Morning

Sara's intentions were to awake early Thursday morning and be on the road by sunrise. She woke when Abbie came through the door calling out a cheerful, "Good morning."

"What time is it?" Sara jumped from the bed.

"Half past nine." Abbie motioned with her hand. "Come into the kitchen. I made you all breakfast."

"Get up, sleepyhead." Sara gave Izzie a shake. "It's late."

"Go away." Izzie turned over and put a pillow over her head.

"Get up or I'll leave you here." Sara shook her again, this time hard. "We should already be on the road."

"I need my rest." Izzie grumbled as she tumbled out of bed.

Sara went into the kitchen. Abbie had made coffee, cooked biscuits, and opened a jar of peach jam for breakfast.

Sara and Izzie ate as Abbie drank coffee and chatted. "You all must promise me you will stop by when you come back through Cactus Gully."

Sara promised, thanked Abbie for her hospitality, and offered to clean the kitchen.

Abbie would hear of no such thing. "You girls get on your way. You have a long drive ahead of you."

The sun was high in the heavens when Sara pulled onto the highway and headed west.

"I had a good time. I never saw anything like those fireworks." Izzie kept up an endless flow of chatter. "All that music. I wish I could play a guitar like the Muddy Bottom River Boys do. Can I tell you a secret?" Without waiting for an answer, she continued. "I have never gone anywhere before. This was my first trip out into the world."

That simple admission stirred sadness inside Sara and brought a wave of shame. Izzie enjoyed simple pleasures she took for granted.

"Did you have fun?" Izzie asked.

Sara shrugged. She did, although she was reluctant to admit it.

"Those church people were so nice. Are all church people like that?"

"I don't know all church people."

"Are all the ones you know nice?"

"Don't confuse church people with Christians." Sara glanced briefly in Izzie's her direction. "There's a difference." She turned her eyes back to the road

"What kind of difference?"

"You should ask your pastor that question." Izzie had raised an issue Sara was uncomfortable trying to explain.

"I don't have a pastor." Izzie's brow wrinkled, and she frowned as if she were deep in thought. After several moments her head came up and her frown was replaced with a smile. "Can I ask your pastor?"

"When we get to the farm you can talk to Moses Gentry. He was my pastor until I left the farm and came to Houston." The acid taste of guilt flooded Sara's mouth. Maybe she should talk to Moses too. Her spiritual life was sadly lacking.

"Do you know how to cook?" Izzie's words intruded into Sara's troubling self-assessment.

"I do. I like to cook." A change of subject matter was a relief. "I like baking best of all."

"Can you bake a pecan pie like the one we had yesterday?"

Sara could, and she said so, with a touch of pride sounding in her voice.

"Will you teach me how?" Izzie leaned forward with a look of hopeful anxiety on her face.

"I don't know if I could." Cooking was one thing. Teaching someone else was another.

"You're just like everybody else." Izzie sat up straight and stared through the windshield. "You think I'm stupid. Well, I'm not. I'm ignorant, but I can learn."

"That's not what I meant." Sara was appalled that Izzie would think such a thing, let alone speak those thoughts aloud. "I was not questioning your ability to learn but my ability to teach." Minutes of silence ticked by before she added. "Yes, I will teach you how to make a pecan pie."

"Thank you, Sara."

Chapter Twenty-One

July 5, 1945
Thursday Afternoon

The nearer she got to the farm, the more excited Sara became. She would see Mama, and Grandma, and Daddy. She had missed them so much. James and Peggy Sue would be there too, and—perish the thought—Junior. She turned off the paved road and onto the rutted lane that was the last lap of the journey home.

"How much farther?" Izzie steadied herself by holding onto the dashboard in front of her.

"Three miles, or near that." Sara slowed the pickup. "Sorry, but the rest of the ride is a bumpy one."

"Do your mama and daddy know I'm coming with you?"

"Mama and Daddy don't know I'm coming."

They rounded a curve. The farmhouse came into view. A sleek bright yellow four-door sedan sat in the driveway beside Daddy's old pickup.

Sara pulled behind Daddy's pickup and stopped. Something was amiss. She could feel it in her bones. Before she could get out, Kent bounded out the front door. He was followed by Mama, James, and Grandma.

"Where have you been?" Kent skidded to a stop and yanked her door handle. "We have half of South Texas looking for you."

James headed for his pickup. "I'll drive into Cedar Gap and tell the sheriff we found her."

"Take my car." Kent pitched James his car keys.

James caught them. "I shouldn't be gone long. Tell Peggy Sue where I went." He got into the yellow sedan and headed for Cedar Gap.

"You, young lady," Kent shook his finger in Sara's face. "Have some explaining to do."

Grandma came to stand beside Kent. "You might near scared us to death."

Mama pushed them both aside. "How could you pull such a stunt? We were about ready to take off looking for you ourselves. Where have you been?"

Sara opened her pickup door forcing Mama to move aside. "I was never lost." She pointed a finger at Kent. "What are you doing here? You told me you were too busy to take even one day off work."

"I couldn't concentrate on work knowing you were driving all this distance alone. I got into the fastest car on the lot and went home, hoping to catch you. You were already gone. I took off, hoping to catch up to you on the road." Kent's hands shook. "I passed everything on that highway. I never saw a sign of you." His voice rose in pitch and volume. "Where were you?"

"Calm down. You're making a mountain out of a molehill. Izzie and I—" Sara looked around. Izzie was nowhere in sight. "Where did that girl go?"

"She ran off down the road." Grandma pointed. "The minute Kent started yelling."

"You scared her away." Sara faced Kent. "Now we have to find *her*." She started in the direction of the road.

Kent followed. "Why did you listen to Mother when she told you to bring Izzie?"

"Because she wouldn't take no for an answer." Sara stopped and waited.

Kent caught up to her. "Haven't I told you a least a dozen times not to pay any attention to anything Mother says?"

"That's easy to say." Sara put both hands on her hips. "It's not so easy to do."

Mama caught up to them. "Stop it, both of you, and concentrate of finding that frightened girl." She put her hands around her mouth and yelled loud enough to be heard in the next county, "Izzie, where are you?"

The answer was resounding silence.

"Nobody's going to hurt you, darling. You are safe here." This time Mama's tone was sweet and not nearly so loud.

"Word of honor?" Izzie crept from behind a tree and stood waiting for a reply.

"Word of honor," Mama echoed. She covered the space separating her from Izzie and put her arms around the trembling girl's shoulders. "I have some sweet tea and cookies in the house." She turned her scurrilous gaze on Sara and Kent. "You two, settle your differences before you come inside. The idea, fussing and yelling at each other like a couple of spoiled brats."

Kent watched Mama and Izzie disappear through the front door before saying, "I demand to know—" He put his hands on Sara's shoulders and pulled her around to face him. "Where have you been?"

"Take your hands off me." Sara shook herself free.

"I'm sorry." Kent ran his hands along the sides of his hair. "I was so afraid something had happened to you. Worry has about driven me out of my mind."

"I'm sorry, too." He had every reason to be upset. "It's a long story. Let's go inside and I will tell you all about it."

"If your mother will allow us inside. She does have a way of nosing into our business."

"*My* mama is nosy?" Sara had tolerated his mother nosing into every phase of their life and Kent dared complain about her mama pointing out the obvious. "What about *your* mother?" She stood with both hands on her hips. "This entire misunderstanding is her fault. If she hadn't insisted I take Izzie along I would never have stopped for the parade, and we would never have met Abbie, or gone to the picnic, or decided to stay for the music or— "

"Here I have been imagining you lying in a ditch, injured and bleeding, or being kidnapped, or tortured and murdered, or worse, and you went to a parade and a picnic?" Kent raised an eyebrow. "I love you, darling." His scowl converted to a grin. He opened his arms.

Sara walked into them. "I had no idea you would follow me."

"Neither did I." Kent pulled her close to him. "I got to work early, set to put in a long day selling used cars. I couldn't. All I could do was think of you, out on that highway, alone. I finally told Father I had to go with you."

"What did your father say?"

He said, 'Ain't it all sorts of grief loving a woman so much?' Then he told me to get on my way before I made a bigger fool of myself than I already had by giving cars away or some such nonsense."

"You can go back now if you need to. Izzie and I can come back tomorrow." She laid her head against his chest. He came because he loved her. She wanted to laugh and to cry. "I'm sorry I scared you."

"You're okay and that's all that counts." He tilted her chin and kissed her.

"Well, if you two ain't something." Mama stood not ten feet away, smiling and shaking her head. "Come on into the house. James should be back soon and we can have supper."

"Dinner in your home is supper in mine" Sara smiled up at her husband. "Let's go." Arm in arm, they followed Mama into the house.

Chapter Twenty-Two

July 7, 1945
Saturday Morning

Sara followed behind Kent as he drove the pickup down the highway toward Houston. The yellow sedan handled like a dream. It was a 1940 model Oldsmobile Custom Eight cruiser with a fully automatic transmission. It didn't even have a clutch. She had been reluctant to drive it but Kent insisted. She would have done anything he asked as a way to compensate for making him worry about her whereabouts for so long. He came because he loved her.

Izzie had been strangely quiet since they left the farm. Sara was too lost into her own thoughts to wonder why, until she asked, "Are we going to stop in Cactus Gulch to see Abbie?"

"Not this time." Sara had forgotten all about Abbie. "Maybe next time we can stop and pay her a visit."

"You promised her we would stop *this* time."

Sara was set to deny that accusation when sudden hindsight brought remembrance. She *had* promised.

"So, can we stop?" Izzie was nothing if not persistent.

"No, we can't. The subject is closed."

"You shouldn't make promises you don't intend to o keep." Izzie twisted in the seat to face Sara. "Why do you?"

"This is a one-time case. There are extenuating circumstances. When I see Abbie, I will explain and apologize." Sara was reaching the end of her rope with Izzie's impertinent questions. She said once again, this time with great emphasis, "The subject is closed."

Izzie was silent for the next few miles.

Sara lapsed, once more, into remembering. This time recalling the events of the day before. Daddy hadn't known who she was. That broke her heart. Mama said not to let it bother her. Sometimes Daddy didn't know who *she* was, and she had been his wife for nearly thirty years.

It did bother Sara, and left her with a lingering sense of guilt. She should be home, helping Mama. She had voiced that thought to James. He was carrying a big load, what with running the farm and Peggy Sue definitely expecting another baby.

James assured her that they were managing fine. He told her that her place was with her husband.

Still, Sara couldn't shake off that persistent, nagging guilt. She would go back to visit them soon.

"Can I ask you a question? It's not about Abbie." Izzie broke Sara's chain of unpleasant thoughts.

"If it's about this car, don't ask. I don't know."

"It's not. Why did you promise me I could talk to Preacher Moses about Jesus if you didn't intend to keep that promise?"

The words struck Sara like a blow to her mid-section. Her conversation with Izzie about knowing Jesus had completely slipped her mind.

Izzie sat with folded hands, patiently waiting for a reply.

"I forgot." She must find some way to make amends for such an unforgiveable oversight. "My house is behind a church. I will arrange for their pastor to talk to you. His name is Pastor Frank. Why didn't you mention this to me while we were still at the farm?"

"Because Mr. Holden was in a hurry and I didn't want him yelling and pointing his finger at me."

"Then everything is settled?"

"Everything," Izzie answered, "except where Pastor Frank will talk to me. He can't come to Mrs. Holden's house. She would pitch a hissy fit to end all hissy fits."

"I'll find a way as soon as I get settled in."

"Do you promise?"

"I promise and this time I won't forget."

July 9, 1945
Monday Morning

The moment Kent left for work, Sara called the transfer company and arranged for two men to meet her at her house around noon. She was glad Martha had insisted they wait until Monday to move in to their house.

Martha also demanded they park the pickup in the garage. "What will people think when the see that rattle-trap loaded with junk sitting in my driveway?"

Sara overlooked the insult and agreed, mostly because the church would look askance at them moving in on Sunday. She loaded the remainder of their belongings into the pickup Sunday afternoon.

Her plan now was to slip out this morning, without Martha knowing, go to a grocery store, and be at her house by eleven.

That was her plan. Like so many other well-laid strategies, it went astray. Martha was waiting for her in the foyer. "Where are you off to in such a hurry?"

"I have a lot to do today."

"That's not what I asked." Martha shook her head. "Surely you aren't thinking of trying to unpack all the junk you have loaded on that pickup by yourself. You must wait until Lester and Kent can help you."

"Everything is taken care of." Sara moved toward the door.

Martha stepped in front of her. "I must talk to you about Izzie."

"Izzie is not my problem." Martha was looking for some way, any way to keep Sara from moving out of this house.

"Don't you want to hear what I have to say?"

"Not especially." Sara stepped around her mother-in-law and hurried through the door.

Martha followed her outside.

Sara raised the garage door and got into the pickup.

Martha came to stand on the passenger side of the vehicle. She laid her arms across the window and stuck her head inside. "Really, Sara—

"If you don't want me to run over you, move." Sara started the engine.

"I am not letting—" Martha didn't budge.

Sara revved the motor.

Her mother-in-law jumped back as she screamed.

Sara took that opportunity to back from the garage and on to the street.

Martha came from the garage, shaking her fist, and screaming obscenities.

Sara sped away. She was shaking like a leaf. She stopped at the corner and pulled to the side of the road. She could have injured Martha or even killed her. *That woman makes me crazy.* Gradually, her heart slowed and she stopped shaking. She started the pickup and drove toward her new home. *I hope I never have to go back to that place again.*

By the time she reached the grocery store, Sara had regained emotional control. Maybe she was the spoiled brat Mama had accused her of being. She had certainly acted like one. She owed Martha an apology. The next time she saw her mother-in-law she would ask for her forgiveness. She bought her groceries and drove home.

The men from the transfer company were waiting for her. They spent the next two hours unloading and setting up furniture.

After the men left, Sara put a beef roast in the oven and straightened the house. She sang as she worked. She and Kent had a place of their own. At last, they could begin their life together.

Doubts returned, as they always did when Sara thought of her life with Kent. The words that distressed her more each time she recalled them were *I don't want children. I have my reasons. On this one subject there is no compromise. Sorry, Sara, but that's the way it is.*

He would change his mind. She would make him. At times like this she wanted Mama's comfort and advice. She wished for Grandma's stories about when she was a young wife. Grandma always began her stories by saying, 'Things were different then.'

Kent came home early. He was pleased with what Sara had done in the house.

"I loved doing it." She put food on the table. Her roast was done to perfection. She also served potatoes she'd cooked with the roast and snapped green peas. For dessert she made a deep-dish peach pie. So what if she used most of their meat and sugar coupons? This was a special occasion.

Kent had nothing but praise for her culinary efforts, telling her that she was as good a cook as Mrs. Mac.

Sara's doubts receded. She was always so sure of their future when she was in Kent's presence.

They retired to the living room. Sara had put Kent's house slippers beside his easy chair. His pipe, tobacco, and the evening edition of the newspaper were on the table to his right.

It was a lovely evening. Kent read his paper and talked about his busy day at work. Sara crocheted and listened. She loved the sound of his voice.

When Kent looked up from his paper and suggested it must be bedtime, she agreed wholeheartedly.

Later, in his arms, she forgot everything but her love for this man.

He whispered, "I love you."

Her heart soared. "I love you too, more than you will ever know."

Later, she drifted into a contented sleep, thinking all was right with her world.

Chapter Twenty-Three

July 13, 1945
Friday Morning

Sara sat at the kitchen table, looking through the recipes she had collected through the years when a knock sounded on the front door. *Who in the world?* She hurried to answer.

Another knock sounded before she could get from the kitchen to the front door. Someone was impatient. She opened the door.

"Hi, Sara." Izzie stood on the other side. "I came to talk to Pastor Frank. Can I come in?"

"Yes, of course." Sara unhooked the screen and held it open. "Does Martha know where you are?"

"Not exactly." Izzie came into the room. "This is nice." Uninvited, she sat on the couch.

"What do you mean by 'Not exactly'?" Sara sat in her newly-upholstered rocking chair. "If you have done something to get me in more trouble with my mother-in-law..." She remembered why Izzie was here and the promises she had made. Her voice softened and she rephrased her question. "Explain what you mean by 'Not exactly.'"

"I told Mrs. Holden this was Friday the 13th. I said there was a hex on me. I always have bad luck on this day. If I dropped dishes, or forgot how to lay the table the way I was supposed to, or if I said supper instead of dinner, messed up in any way, she would have to forgive me, because it was that old hex working."

"Did she believe you?" More than once Izzie had told Sara she wasn't stupid. Sara had dismissed it as idle talk. Her opinion of the girl was beginning to change.

"I don't know." Izzie shrugged her indifference. "Anyway, she told me to leave and not to come back until tomorrow. She said I would have to make it up by working Sunday. I came here instead of going to my Mama's house because I want to know about Jesus."

A half-dozen conflicting emotions converged inside Sara. Izzie told a blatant lie. She did it because she wanted more information about Jesus. It was information she had asked Sara for twice before. Each time she put the girl off with some lame excuse. She should have been thankful for the opportunity to witness for her Savior. She would have, but she was busy with her own problems. That was a poor excuse and she knew it.

"Can we go now?" Izzie sat on the edge of the couch and waited for Sara's answer.

"Now is as good a time as any." Sara stood and untied her apron. "Let's go."

"What if Pastor Frank doesn't want to talk to me?" Izzie followed Sara out the front door.

"He will," Sara assured her.

"You wouldn't."

"Do you want to see Pastor Frank or not?" Sara closed the door and hurried down the walk toward the street.

"Haven't I told you that's why I came here?" Izzie followed along behind her.

Surely the good pastor would be at his home. Didn't all pastors begin studying for Sunday sermons early Friday morning? Moses said they did, if they were dedicated to their calling.

They went first to the house nearest the church. The old woman who answered the door told them the pastor and his family lived across the street. She opened her screen and pointed. "Right over there."

Sara thanked her and she and Izzie went to the house the old woman indicated. A young and very attractive woman answered the door. When Sara told her they were looking for Pastor Frank she said he was at the church. Sara thanked her, and the two of them were off again.

They stepped into the church foyer to see a man sweeping the auditorium. Sara called to him. "Can you tell us where to find Pastor Frank?"

"You're looking at him." The man straightened and smiled. He was short and misshapen. His head was too large for his body and his arms and legs were inordinately short. His hair was the color of copper. His face was round as a new moon, and splattered with freckles.

He's a dwarf. "We would like a word with you, if that's possible."

"How can I help you?" He laid his push broom aside and came toward them.

"He's a freak," Izzie screeched, as she moved to stand behind Sara who was embarrassed beyond measure.

"He is not." She yanked Izzie's arm, forcing the frightened girl to stand, once
more, beside her. "He's a dwarf." Her face burned with humiliation. "Please forgive us. We meant no disrespect. It's just— "

"Forget it, I've been called worse. Let me introduce myself." The pastor extended his hand. "I'm Pastor Frank Evans."

"*You* are the preacher who is going to tell me about Jesus?" Izzie most reluctantly shook his short, chubby hand.

"If that is your wish." Pastor Frank smiled. "Fortunately for me, God looks at
the inner man."

Sara's face still burned. She was completely mortified. She searched for her
voice, but it had deserted her. She shook Pastor Frank's hand. He must think
she was a complete idiot.

Not so with Izzie. The handshake seemed to expel her fears. "My name is Izzie."
She pointed to Sara. "This is Sara. She lives in the house behind your church.
She won't tell me about Jesus, but she says you will."

"Izzie, please." Another wave of heat bathed Sara's face. "I'll wait outside." Sara
moved toward the back pew.

"I must insist that you accompany us." Pastor Frank came into the vestibule,
took a ring of keys from his pocket, and unlocked the door to his right. It was
marked Pastor's Study. "I try always to maintain the utmost propriety. Izzie is
so young. She needs someone with her as we talk about this most important of
subjects."

Sara nodded her head in agreement. Put that way, how could she refuse?

Pastor Frank held the office door open and stood aside. The room was small and
sparsely furnished, but neat. A battered old desk stood along one wall. Across
from it was a bookcase filled with books that showed marks of being read and
reread.

Sara entered slowly. Izzie followed her. Pastor Frank waddled along behind
them. He closed the door and moved to sit on a stool behind his desk.

Izzie and Sara sat in two straight-backed chairs that were placed strategically in
front of the pastor's desk.

"She," Izzie pointed toward Sara, "says there's a difference between church people and Christians. She wouldn't tell me what that difference is. Maybe she doesn't know. She said you would tell me."

"That's not what I said." Sara twisted in her chair.

"You did so." Izzie's voice rose in indignation. "You said—"

"It's not what I said, exactly." An admonition Grandma often advocated ran through Sara's brain: *Tell the truth and shame the devil.* "If I did, that's not what I meant."

"Ladies, ladies, never mind." Pastor Frank lifted one hand and waved it from side to side. "It's not important who said what. Shall we get on with what you came here to discuss?" Under his breath he added, "Whatever that is."

"I talked to Izzie about being a Christian." Sara defended herself. Izzie's explanation cast her in a bad light.

"You did not." Izzie was on the defensive and determined to have the last word.

"Never mind." Pastor Frank's voice carried a hint of impatience. "Miss Izzie, let's talk about the Lord Jesus." He picked up the Bible that lay on his desk. "Do you know what book this is?"

"Yes, sir, I do. It's a Bible."

"Do you know what's in it?"

"No, sir. I don't."

"Have you ever read any of it?"

"No, sir, I haven't. I did go to vacation Bible school once, when I was ten years old."

A lump rose in Sara's throat. How far short she fell from the Christian witness she should be.

Pastor Frank lifted the book that lay open before him. "The Bible is God's word. It is divided into two sections. In each section are books. Each book contains chapters divided into verses." Pastor Frank opened his bible, and turned it toward Izzie. "This Bible is opened to the section called the New Testament. The book you are looking at is The Gospel of John. Can you show me chapter three?" He laid it back on his desk.

Izzie scooted her chair nearer, leaned forward, and pulled the Bible toward her. She studied it for several minutes before pointing to chapter three.

"Very good." Pastor Frank's round face broke into a smile. "Can you find verse sixteen?"

"I can try." Izzie ran her forefinger down the page, and up the second column until she found verse sixteen. "It's right here."

"Very good, now read it to me."

Sara read in Izzie's expression the intent to refuse. She was set to offer encouragement. A power stronger than her own stopped her. A still-small voice whispered inside her head. *Be still, and listen to the Word."* She sat silent and attentive.

"For God so loved the world," Izzie paused.

"You're doing great," Pastor Frank assured her. "Read on."

"For God so loved the world, that he gave his only—" Once more she paused. "I don't know what 'begotten' means."

"Let me offer a substitute and finish the reading." Pastor Frank turned the Bible in his direction and read slowly and distinctly:

> *For God so loved the world, that he gave his one and only son, that whosoever believes in him, shall not die, but have eternal life. John 3:16*

Chapter Twenty-Four

July 13, 1945
Friday Morning

Sara listened as Pastor Frank explained God's wonderful plan of salvation. Why couldn't she articulate these sweet and simple words? How miserably she had failed in her Christian life. She was still a babe in Christ, and worse yet, an ungrateful babe. She had accepted all God's wonderful blessings in her life as if they were her due. She had never sought to work for and praise Him. *God be merciful to me, your undone and unthankful child. I rededicate my life to You. Help me, from this day forward, to serve and honor You.*

"Why didn't somebody tell me about Jesus a long time ago?" Tears stood in Izzie's eyes.

"I wonder the same thing." Pastor Frank took a handkerchief from his pocket and gave it to Izzie. "There are so many lost souls are all around us." His eyes met Sara's, causing her to drop her head and stare at the floor. "And yet we, as Christians, never notice or think to speak to them."

"I want to pray to Jesus now." Izzie wiped her eyes and smiled through her still flowing tears. "I want to ask Him to come into my heart, forgive me of my sins, and always be with me."

"We will all pray. Let us bow our heads." Pastor Frank closed his Bible. "Sara, would you pray first?"

Being asked to pray was the last thing Sara expected. She closed her eyes and spoke her heart. "Thank You God, for your many blessings. Hear my repentant prayer. Forgive me for the many ways I have failed you. Show me the pathway to spiritual maturity. Help—" She could say no more. A lump rose in her throat.

Pastor Frank took up where she left off. He prayed a sweet prayer of praise. He closed by thanking God for sending Sara and Izzie to him. He nodded in Izzie's direction.

She prayed a prayer that touched Sara's heart, thanking and praising God for sending His son to be her savior.

Pastor Frank's "Amen" closed the session.

Sara had never before been so moved. She lifted her head and smiled at Izzie, who returned her smile. Neither of them spoke. Words weren't necessary.

"Can I count on the two of you being in church somewhere this Sunday?" Pastor Frank slid from his stool and stood.

"I will be at church." Izzie shook his extended hand. "I want to know more about Jesus."

"So will I," Sara said, as she, in turn, shook Pastor Frank's hand. Would Kent come with her? She didn't know. She did know that her repentance and commitment stood firm. Beginning this day, she would study the word, serve her lord, and grow in His grace and knowledge. She would win Kent over. With Jesus' help, he would be in church at her side this Sunday and every Sunday thereafter.

July 14, 1945
Saturday Evening

"Dinner was delicious." Kent leaned back in his easy chair and lit his pipe. "You've done wonders decorating this house. Who taught you to be such a great homemaker?"

"Mama taught me to cook. Grandma taught me to sew and do handwork." How handsome he was with the glow from the floor lamp casting a halo of light around his head and accentuating his chiseled features. *I love you, Kent Holden.* "I must remember to thank them both the next time I see them."

"Izzie was here yesterday." Sara picked up her embroidery.

"Father spoke of Izzie over lunch today," Kent said. "He said she was worried about some foolish Friday the 13th hex."

"What do you really know about Izzie?" Sara kept her eyes on her sewing.

"Not much, why?"

"She's such an enigma. I took her to see Reverend Frank. He pastors the church that owns this house."

"Why would you do that?" Kent sat up and laid his pipe aside. "Surely you don't believe her story about a Friday the 13th hex."

"I do not and neither does Izzie." Sara laid her stitchery aside and faced her husband's bewildered gaze. "She wanted yesterday off. That story assured her of getting it."

"I still don't understand."

"How old were you when you first heard the story of Jesus?" Sara once more picked up her embroidery. She needed something to occupy her hands.

"I don't remember, exactly." Kent looked more confused by the minute. "It was long before I started to school. What does that have to do with Izzie and her lie about thinking she is hexed?"

Sara explained about her conversation with Izzie as they drove to the farm. "She wanted me to tell her the difference between a church member and a Christian. I felt inadequate to do that. I promised instead to take her to someone who could. She showed up yesterday morning asking me to make good on that promise." Sara stopped her sewing and looked up. "That's what I did."

"This seems to me to be a tempest in a tea pot. If there is a difference it must be minimal." Kent picked up his paper as if that settled the matter.

"Surely you don't believe that." Sara was shocked. "There is a world of difference."

"Such as?" Kent cut his eyes in her direction.

"Some people join a church because they think being a member will make them a better person. Some join for social reasons, some to please family members, or—"

"Do you want to know what I *really* believe?" Kent gave his paper a flip before folding it and laying it on the table beside his chair.

"I do." A lead weight settled in Sara's stomach. *At least. I think I do.*

"I don't believe God gives a hang about what happens on this earth below, good or bad."

"That's not true." His words rang in her ears like some trumpet of doom. "God loves his children. He watches over and cares for them."

Kent jumped from his chair and strode across the room before turning to face her. "Tell me, then, why I spent four years of my life in hell. I saw rape and pillage, destruction and devastation. After the second offensive, I lost count of how many men I killed, I even—" He stopped and took a deep breath. "Never mind. I can't undo it, and neither can God." He put his head in his hands and wept bitterly.

"Oh, my poor darling." Sara jumped from her place on the couch, and ran toward him. She put her arms around his waist and laid her head on his chest. "That's all behind you now." She heard the rapid beat of his heart as she held him close. What terrible things had he witnessed? What dreadful acts had he been forced to perform, just to survive?

"It's in the past, yes, but the memories will always be with me."

"They will fade with time." She called after him as he walked back to his chair and sat down, the very picture of dejection.

"We can go to church tomorrow and ask God to help us." Sara sat on the couch as dread caught in her throat, making it hard for her to breath. "He will. I know He will.

"You don't understand." Kent's shoulders slumped, as if the weight of the world rested on them. "I no longer have a place in God's scheme of things. My only reality now is you." His voice took on a far-away, surrealistic quality. "You who are so untouched by the baser elements of this world. So innocent, so trusting, my light in a world of endless darkness." His eyes locked into hers. They were tawny brown and hard as agate. "Promise you will never leave me."

Sara grasped one hand in another. How could she be his strength when she was so weak and needy herself?

"If you love me, you will promise me."

"I promise." Sara gasped and swallowed. *God, please help you little sparrow on her house top, so alone and afraid.*

Chapter Twenty-Five

July 15, 1945
Sunday Evening

Sara sat at her kitchen table, drinking a glass of tea, and wondered where Kent could be. He left before she went to church this morning. She had thought he would be home when she returned at noon. He wasn't.

Last evening after his outburst, he sat staring into space. Sara continued her embroidering. She wanted to say so many things. Discretion dictated she hold her tongue. Just when she thought she could not bear another minute of silence, he spoke, asking her forgiveness for his outburst. "It won't happen again."

The arctic quality of his voice was like a slammed door. A knot lodged in her throat and tears filled her eyes, blinding her. The needle she pushed through her sewing went deep into her finger. Tiny drops of crimson bled out onto the white of her pillow slip. She cried out in pain, dropped her sewing, and stuck her finger in her mouth.

"What have I done now?" Kent came to sit beside her. "My poor darling."

This morning before he left, he was his old self. Sara wanted to bring up last night's conversation. Once more silence seemed the better option. Now, as shadows fell, signaling the coming night, she wondered if she had made the right choice.

"Sara?" Kent came through the front door, calling her name.

"I'm in the kitchen."

"I hope you haven't made dinner because I brought barbeque and all the trimmings." He stood in the doorway carrying a big brown paper bag.

"I haven't." Dinner had been the farthest thing from her mind. It was on the tip of her tongue to ask him where he had been. Once again, she chose discretion.

"This is the best barbeque in Texas." Kent set the bag on the table.

"I have iced tea in the refrigerator." Sara laid the table and they sat down.

The barbeque was delicious. They ate in companionable silence.

What were Kent's thoughts? Where had he been all day? Sara pushed back her plate and sighed.

"How was your day?" Kent asked as he stood and stacked dishes.

"It was pleasant, but I missed having you home." She put food into the refrigerator.

They did the dishes. Sara washed. Kent dried. Their conversation was sparse and trivial until Kent said, "I am having a telephone installed tomorrow. I want to be able to call you during the day. Would you like that?"

"Can we afford such a luxury?"

"A telephone is not a luxury. It's a necessity, and yes, we can afford it." Kent hung his dish towel on a hanger near the sink. "My question was, would you like having a telephone?"

"I don't know. I never had a phone before." Sara followed Kent into the living room and sat on the couch.

"Not even in Beaumont?" Kent sank into his easy chair.

"No."

"Now you will." He tamped tobacco into the bowl of his pipe. "The directory listing will be in the name of Mr. and Mrs. Kent Holden."

"That will be nice." Sara picked up her embroidery. Two bright red spots of blood marred the pattern of her stitches. "I don't know anyone to call, but knowing you will call me is nice."

"You can call Mother." He puffed on his pipe. "She's expecting an apology from you. She refused to tell me what the apology should be for."

"I do owe her an apology." Sara put her sewing in her lap as she recalled their last meeting. "We had quite a set-to before I left last Monday."

"Are you sure it isn't the other way around, and she is the one who should apologize to you?"

"Last Monday I would have agreed with you." Sara smiled as she remembered her rededicating her life to serving God. "Things are different now. I am responsible for my own behavior and my conduct last Monday was inexcusable."

"It will be easier to apologize on the telephone." Kent picked up his paper and shook it open.

"I will call her as soon as we get the phone." She couldn't help but ask, "Did you have a good day?"

"So-so." He shrugged. "I would rather have spent it with you."

"You could have come home. I was here, alone all afternoon. Where were you, what did you do?" She sounded like a nagging wife.

"I worked most of the morning at the dealership, catching up on paperwork. I met Mother and Father for lunch. They took me to a very classy restaurant. Ariel was there with a friend. Mother invited them to join us. Afterward, Ariel and her friend invited me to go with them to a concert in the park. I spent the remainder of the afternoon sitting on a blanket, listening to classical music."

Sara saw Martha's fine hand in this meeting of Kent and his first wife. Words her mother-in-law had spoken about Ariel danced across her troubled mind. *Ariel has blond hair. She is tall and very curvy.* "I didn't know you liked classical music."

"I don't, especially. Ariel and I spent most of the time arguing about how soon Japan will surrender."

"What did you decide?" He had spent Sunday afternoon with his first wife, listening to classical music and discussing when Japan would surrender while she sat at home, alone, worrying about where he was.

"We didn't," Kent admitted as he sighed. "I don't think they will last until August. Last month Norway and Italy declared war on them. The Australians have captured Borneo. We are bombing their major cities— "

"What does Ariel think?" Sara struggled to keep sarcasm from her voice.

"Ariel thinks they will hold out for at least three more months." If he noticed her disdain, he didn't show it. "When did we ever agree on anything? She loves disputing what I say and if possible winning the argument."

Sara lapsed into morose silence. There seemed nothing else to say. She folded her handwork and put it in her sewing basket beside the couch.

"Would you like to go for a walk?" Kent folded his paper and laid it on the table.

"I'm going to bed." Sara stood.

"Can you sleep so soon after that big meal?"

"I will read awhile." Was he so stupid that he didn't realize her anger bubbled just below the surface?

"I'll be back soon." He brushed his lips across her cheek, and went through the front door, closing it carefully behind him.

Chapter Twenty-Six

August 8, 1945
Wednesday Morning

Sara was beginning to wonder if she could be both a good Christian and a good wife. She continued to attend church each Sunday morning. Kent continued to disappear early and remain gone until dinnertime. She went to the Wednesday afternoon ladies Bible study, but skipped attending Sunday evening services, even though she felt that was where she should be. Kent refused to listen to anything that remotely hinted of religion. Sara no longer asked him where he went or what he did on Sundays.

She made a special effort to be loving and tender toward her husband. She prayed, asking God for guidance. No answer came. Her guilt and indecision were tearing her apart.

She and Kent were drifting farther and farther away from each other. They went out, on occasion. They visited Lester and Martha. Their love life was passionate and satisfying, but the closeness she felt with him was gone and she knew why. He was determined to distance himself from anything even slightly related to God. She had rededicated her life to love and serve Him.

She opened her Bible to Matthew chapter six, the chapter the ladies Bible class would be studying this afternoon. The last two verses hung like burrs in her mind.

But seek ye first the kingdom of God, and his righteousness; and all these things shall be added unto you.

Take therefore no thought for the morrow: for the morrow shall take thought for the things of itself. Sufficient unto the day is the evil thereof. Matthew 6: 33, 34 KJV

Deep in her heart, she had known the answer all along. She must put God first. The question now was, if seeking God and His kingdom meant losing Kent, could she do it? She didn't know. She honestly didn't know. *Sufficient unto the day is the evil thereof.* She would think about it tomorrow.

August 11, 1945
Saturday Morning

Two tomorrows had come and gone and Sara was no nearer finding answers to her dilemma than she was on Wednesday. She wished for Mama and Grandma to guide and comfort her, but they were almost two hundred miles away.

She looked at her newly-installed telephone and was tempted to call Kent, and ask him if they might have lunch together and talk. About what? A crowded restaurant with limited time was not the place to begin a discussion of the problems that lay between them.

The thought came to her like a bolt from the blue. "I can talk to Pastor Frank's wife." Without further thought, she grabbed her purse and keys, and hurried toward the front door.

She was climbing the porch steps of the parsonage when it occurred to her that she should have called first. It was too late now. She crossed the porch and knocked on the door.

The eldest Evans son, who was a smaller image of his father, answered.

"Good morning, Daniel. Is your mother home?" His appearance always startled Sara. Why would God give the Evans two dwarfs and three normal children? She knew she shouldn't question the Almighty's decisions, but sometimes she did. This was one of those times.

"Yes, ma'am, Mrs. Holden." He opened the door wide and unlatched the screen. "Won't you come in? Mama's in the kitchen, I'll fetch her."

Sara stepped into the neat living room as Irene Frank came from the kitchen, wiping her hands on her apron as she entered. "Mrs. Holden, what a pleasant surprise. Won't you sit down?" She nodded to the slim teenage girl who followed her into the room. ""Clara, dear, turn off the burners on the stove."

"I'm interrupting your cooking." Sara moved toward the door. "I should have called first."

"Nonsense." Irene pointed to a chair and sat on one end of the couch. "Come back here and sit down."

"I apologize for coming without an appointment or an invitation." Sara perched on the chair, feeling embarrassed and unsure.

"Relax, Sara. I can call you Sara?"

"Oh, please do."

"And you must call me Irene." She leaned back and sighed. "Now that the formalities are over, would you like to tell me why you are here?"

"I need someone to talk to, someone I can trust. Mama and Grandma are back on the farm. That's so far away, almost two hundred miles." She paused, as tears filled her eyes. "I am babbling like an idiot. I don't know what to do."

"Come sit here." Irene patted the cushion beside her. "We can pray about this."

"I have prayed." Sara moved to the couch and dug in her purse for a handkerchief. "I have prayed and prayed." She wiped her eyes. "I don't know if there is an answer to my problem."

"There's always an answer." Irene took Sara's hand. "It may not always be the answer we want, but there is an answer." She bowed her head. "Let's pray."

A tiny short-limbed, large–headed child toddled into the room. She was pursued by Clara, who caught up to her as she waddled toward her mother. "I'm sorry, Mama, I thought she was with the boys."

"Come to Mama, Leona." Irene held out her arms, scooped up the child and sat her on her lap. "It's all right, Clara." She nodded toward the girl.

"I should go. I am interrupting your routine." Sara's self-pity evaporated to be replaced by sympathy for this beautiful woman.

"I don't have a routine." Irene kissed the top of her little daughter's curly head as she smiled. "Five children and a pastor for a husband make that impossible." She sat a squirming Leona on the floor. "I'm not complaining, mind you, just stating facts."

Leona toddled away, swinging her arms, and singing *Jesus Loves Me* as she went. Once more Irene took Sara's hand. "Before each of my children was born, I prayed they would be normal size. Three times God granted me what I asked for. Twice the answer was no. He taught me a great lesson by saying no to me twice. Daniel and Leona are two of the greatest blessings in my life. I have learned to ask God to have His will in my life, and then to give me the grace to accept what He wills. Would you like to talk about your problem?"

Sara would, and she did, but with a humility she had not felt in a long time.

Chapter Twenty-Seven

September 2, 1945
Monday Morning

Sara cleared away the breakfast dishes. She looked forward to today. Lester was hosting a Labor Day picnic in the park for the employees of the car dealership. Since her talk last month with Irene, she had come to accept Kent's attitude, and to deal with it on a daily basis. The evening after her visit with Irene, she talked to him. He listened, and shrugged when she explained her commitment to God, and how she must honor it. "I will be attending morning and evening church services each Sunday hereafter." Sunday evening, she attended church services. She hardly heard the sermon. Her mind was on Kent, and how he would react to her ultimatum.

He acted true to form by surprising her and never broaching the subject again. He did continue to disappear early each Sunday morning, and not return home until late in the evening.

The ringing telephone interrupted her disquieting thoughts. She raced to answer.

Kent lifted the receiver as she came into the living room. "Hello." His deep voice vibrated through the room. "Yes." After a long silence. "I can take a message." After a longer silence, he whispered. "Thank you," and hung up.

"Who was that?" She could tell the call had not brought good tidings.

"It was the owner of the feed store in Cedar Gap." Kent took her in his arms and held her close. "Your family sent word in by Moses this morning early. They wanted him to ask the feed store manager to call you."

"What happened?" Cold crept down Sara's backbone and lodged in her stomach.

"It's your father. He left the house Saturday night. They didn't miss him until Sunday morning. They found him early this morning in your stock tank. He drowned."

Her brain tried to translate the words she was hearing. Like stones across water, they skipped over her thoughts. Her heart refused to accept what her mind knew was true.

Kent led her to the couch and sat beside her. He put his arms around her, and pulled her close. "I'm so sorry, my darling, so sorry."

"I have to go there. Mama needs me." She should shed tears. She would if she could find some to shed.

"I'll take you." He smoothed her hair with his hand, "I'll call Father and tell him we will be out of town for a few days."

"I'll pack a bag." Sara stood. The world moved in slow motion. Her head spun.

"You're in shock." Kent pushed her back down onto the couch. "I'll do the packing after I call Father. We should be on our way within the hour." He picked up the telephone.

*****

September 2, 1945
Monday Afternoon

They left in less than an hour, but not before Sara called Irene and asked for the church to pray for them on their journey, and for help and guidance through the ordeal that lay ahead of them. Irene expressed her sympathy and promised the church's prayers.

Kent listened as she talked to Irene. He didn't say a word. He expressed his displeasure by scowling and pressing his lips together.

Obviously, Kent had claimed the Oldsmobile Custom Eight cruiser as his own. He was still driving it. They traveled for some time in complete silence. Sara was lost in her own thoughts. Daddy was gone. He was dead. What a terrible ring the word *dead* carried. Old memories crept in. Daddy teaching her how to ride a horse. Daddy telling her bedtime stories. Daddy teaching her a bedtime prayer. The tears that had so far eluded her, burst forth with sudden force. They were wrenching sobs, impossible to control, dreadful to hear. "I don't have a daddy anymore."

"Go ahead, cry." Kent pulled to the side of the road and stopped the car before taking her in his arms. "Tears will help."

"Tears won't bring Daddy back." Her daddy was gone and he would never come back. Sara wiped her eyes on the tail of her dress.

"Be grateful for the time you had with him. I never had a daddy."

"You had Lester." His words ran through Sara like an electric shock. "You still do and he adores you."

"Lester is my father, and I love him. But he's not my daddy, and he never was." Never before had he spoken his heart to her so sincerely. "Tell me the difference. I don't understand."

"The difference is blood." She heard the sadness in his voice. "I'm not a part of Father the way you are a part of your daddy. I don't know who I'm a part of. Who is my daddy? Is he still alive? Did he give me away? Does he even know I exist?"

"Did you ever look for him, or for your mama?" How little she understood about this man she loved so dearly.

"It's not your problem." He started his car and pulled onto the highway. "Forget I mentioned it."

"Anything that is your problem is my problem too." Why couldn't he understand that?

"You have enough on your mind."

Sara learned more about her husband in those few telling minutes than she had known in all their time together. She moved nearer to him, feeling a closeness of spirit that spoke to her heart.

Another truth dawned. There was more than one kind of closeness. This closeness of spirit was different from physical closeness. This revelation was something she felt a need to ponder further.

Chapter Twenty-Eight

September 6, 1945
Thursday Morning

In times to come Sara would look back and wonder how she made it through the next three days. Burying her daddy was the hardest thing she had ever done. Now her concern was for her mother.

James had cleared the living room of everyone except her and Mama. His plea before doing so rang in her ears. *Mama blames herself for Daddy's death. Will you talk to her?*

Had anyone but James asked this of her, she would have said no. How could she refuse the request of her brother after all he had been through? He had borne the brunt of caring for the family through Daddy's illness when she was miles away. He was going to be a father himself in a few months. His time should have been spent preparing for this joyous event and spending time with Peggy Sue. Was it guilt she felt? She drew a deep breath.

Mama sat on the couch and folded her hands in her lap. "Do you and James think I'm too dumb to see what you are up to? Go ahead, say it, and get it off your chest."

"James says you feel responsible for Daddy's death." Why should she beat around the bush? "That's a foolish notion. You must put it from your mind." Sara braced herself for Mama's sharp retort.

"Do you know how many nights I slept beside your daddy?" A tear sounded in Mama's voice. Before Sara could answer, she continued. "I don't. How many nights are there in thirty years? I always knew if he turned over. I heard him when he snored. Why, then, didn't I know when he got out of bed and left the house?"

"Because you were too tired from caring for him all day. Because you weren't supposed to know." *Dear Jesus, give me the words to say.* Sara moved across the room to sit beside her mother. "Remember when I was a little girl and asked you if grass would be green in heaven?"

"I remember," Mama replied. "You were good at asking questions I couldn't answer."

"Do you remember what you told me?" Sara took her mother's hand.

"I said I didn't know, and then I told you there are some things we aren't supposed to know. I said if we knew everything, faith wouldn't be necessary."

"It was Daddy's time to go. That's all we need to know." Sara squeezed her mother's hand. "We accept that by faith, and ask no more. Can you do that, Mama?"

"I can try." Tears rolled down Dora's cheeks as she collapsed in her daughter's arms. "What will I ever do without him? He was the other half of me."

"You will get through this, Mama. I wish I could tell you how you will be able to, but I can't, because I don't know." Sara held her mother close. "I do know this much. With God's help you will make it. We all will make it, with God's help."

"Oh, my child, how little you know about love and marriage." Mama pulled free of Sara's embrace and sat straight and stiff. "I will never get over this. I may get through it, but my life will never be the same again. Thank you for trying." She stood. "It's time I saw to dinner."

Sara caught her mother's arm. "Peggy Sue and Grandma will see to that."

"This is my home." Very gently Dora removed Sara's hand. "Seeing to meals is my duty."

"But Mama," Sara protested.

"I will make it by doing each day, the next thing, and the next—"

How wise her mother was. How much she understood about the human heart. Sara followed her mother into the kitchen.

September 8, 1945
Saturday Morning

"You could have stayed a while longer." Kent glanced briefly in Sara's direction before turning from the dirt road onto the highway.

"I offered," Sara answered. "Mama told me to go home with my husband because that was where I belonged. I argued, but she said my being there wouldn't bring Daddy back or ease her pain."

"James talked to me at length about his parents." Kent passed a slow-moving wagon loaded with hay. "He said they were always very devoted to each other."

"They were." Tears filled Sara's eyes. "They knew each other all their lives. Daddy loved to tease Mama by telling James and me that Mama chased him until he finally caught her. Mama pretended to be mad, but really she was pleased."

"You're crying." Kent slowed behind an eighteen-wheeler. "Does it bother you to talk about your family?"

"No." Sara wiped away her tears with her fingertips. "I love my family and I am flattered James and Peggy Sue are going to name their baby Sara Sue if it's a girl. Sara Sue, I think that's a lovely name."

"I hope Father's Labor Day picnic went well." Kent stiffened. His voice was as cold as an Arctic storm.

"Kent, what is wrong?"

"What makes you think something is wrong with me?" He pushed down on the accelerator and sped around the eighteen-wheeler.

"For starters, you're driving like a crazy man." Sara held onto the dashboard. "Slow down."

He pulled in front of the eighteen-wheeler and continued at breakneck speed. What had she done? What had she said? The answer flashed through her mind like a bolt of chained lightning. The mention of James and Peggie Sue's coming baby was what set him off. Why would speaking about Peggy Sue's pregnancy upset him so?

Sara sat silent and puzzled as gradually Kent slowed to a decent speed.

"I'm sorry." He spoke, breaking the uncomfortable silence. "I don't know what got into me."

"Was it something I said?"

"No, of course not. Let's forget about it, shall we?" He slowed as they came to the city-limits of a small town. "Would your family be offended if I had a telephone installed at the farm?"

"Can we afford to do that?" Would he never cease to amaze her?

"Of course we can, and you could call them often. I know you are especially concerned about your mother."

"Long distant calls are expensive, but it would be nice to call once a week, just to see how they are doing." She used her forefinger to make an X across her heart. "I promise to call only once a week."

"Consider it done, and you can call as often as you please. I'll get in touch with James and make the arrangements." They drove down the main street of the little town. Kent pointed to a café. "How about we stop and have that second cup of coffee?"
"I'd like that."

Chapter Twenty-Nine

November 22, 1945
Thursday Morning

Today was Thanksgiving Day, so declared by President Harry S. Truman. Sara and Kent arrived at Lester and Martha's home just in time for dinner.

Sara would have preferred to go to the church's Thanksgiving service and prepare her own Thanksgiving dinner. Since her apology to her mother-in-law last September, things were better between them. That didn't mean they were good by any stretch of the imagination.

Kent's kindness to and concern for her family made Sara ashamed of her attitude toward his mother. She was appalled when she learned he paid a hefty price to have a telephone line stretched several miles to reach the farm. Once again, she resolved to ignore Martha's snide remarks and demanding ways.

Martha met them at the door. "Do come in. You are just in time. Mrs. Mac prepared a magnificent Thanksgiving meal. It is now being served."

The trio entered the dining room.

Upon seeing Sara, Izzie set a dish on the table, and shouted a greeting. "Hi, Sara. How are you doing?" Her voice dropped to normal. "I'm studying my Bible every day. A seminary student is helping me. We are almost through the book of Numbers. It makes a lot more sense when I have a teacher to guide me—"

"Izzie, really." Martha rapped her spoon on the side of the table. "Remember your place and continue with your duties."

Izzie turned toward the kitchen, mumbling under her breath as she went.

"That child will never learn." Martha expelled a theatrical sigh. "I try. I do try." She paused before asking, "Why is my life so difficult? First presidents keep changing the date for Thanksgiving. Now Izzie forgets everything I have told her. Politicians are useless and that girl is so stupid."

"Izzie is not stupid." The words were out before Sara could stop them. She was doing the very thing she had sworn not to do, disagreeing with her mother-in-law. "That is to say, she doesn't appear stupid to me."

"What do you think, Son?" Martha was not about to let go.

"I think I can solve this problem in short order." Kent stood and headed for the kitchen.

Where was he going? What was he going to do? Sara pushed back her chair got up, and followed him.

He was speaking to Mrs. Mac. She recognized their voices. She couldn't comprehend what they were saying. She moved a little closer and paused in the doorway.

Kent stood across the table from Mrs. Mac. Sara forgot to listen to what they were saying. She was struck by their profiles, so much alike that it startled her. The same hairline, the same shape of the ears, the same long, straight nose. Why had she never noticed before? She gasped.

Kent turned and smiled at her. "You slipped up on us. I was asking Mrs. Mac to keep Izzie in the kitchen."

"I can do that." Mrs. Mac turned to face Sara. Now the resemblance was less noticeable. Had it not been for those two sets of soft-as-velvet brown eyes, she might have thought she was imagining things. Kent's eyes were identical to Mrs. Mac's, not only in color, but in shape and size.

"Are you all right?" He rushed to Sara's side. "You're pale as a ghost."

"I'm okay." Sara reached for Kent's hand as she addressed Mrs. Mac. "This is my fault. I opened my mouth when I should have kept it shut. I'm sorry."

"Don't give it a second thought." Mrs. Mac's smile was benevolent. "You two go ahead and enjoy your Thanksgiving meal. I can see after Izzie."

Sara returned to the table still holding onto Kent's hand. She gritted her teeth and apologized to Martha. "I butted in where I had no business. Please forgive me."

"You certainly did, but of course, I forgive you. It's not in my nature to hold grudges."

Sara thought so many things. She said nothing.

Dinner was finished without further interruption.

After their meal, Lester suggested they play a game of forty-two. "I'll set up the card table and get the dominos."

Sara usually enjoyed playing forty-two. Today her mind kept wandering back to Kent and Mrs. Mac, and the resemblance in their profiles. *And those eyes—*

"Honestly, Sara." Martha's reprimand disturbed Sara's wandering thoughts. "You just gave this hand away. I refuse to be your partner any longer. Lester can be your partner. He's almost as bad a player as you are."

"Now, Mother, that's not nice," Lester complained, but he switched chairs with his wife.

"Stop complaining and shuffle the dominoes." Martha settled in the chair Lester had vacated.

Sara made an effort to concentrate, but try as she night, she could not keep her mind on the game.

After several hands, all of which Lester and Sara lost, Martha called a halt, declaring Lester and Sara had tied for the worst forty-two players in Texas. She stood and pushed her hand against the small of her back. "I am getting old." She nodded toward the kitchen. "Come along, Lester. I will have Mrs. Mac pack some of the leftover food for Kent and Sara to take home with them."

"Mother, you're not old." Lester put dominoes into a box. "Women your age are in the prime of life."

"Stop with the sweet talk and come along." Martha walked away, calling over her shoulder, "You can make yourself useful as well as ornamental."

Lester slapped a lid on the box. "If I didn't love that woman so much, I would leave her first thing tomorrow morning." He trailed along after his wife.

"Pssst." Izzie stuck her head around the corner.

"Izzie?" Sara turned in her chair.

"Is the coast clear?" Izzie crept into the room. "I don't want Mrs. Holden to catch me." She sat in the chair next to Sara. "I need your help. Can I come to see you next Sunday after church? I'll come while Mr. Holden is here visiting his Mama and Daddy."

So this was where Kent spent his Sundays. "Does he bring anyone with him?"

"No. Can I come?"

"Does anyone else show up after he gets here?"

"Like who? Can I come?"

"Like one or both of his ex-wives?"

"No. Nobody else shows up. Will you answer my question?"

"I'd love to have you visit me."

"Okay." The sound of approaching footsteps was enough to send Izzie scurrying for cover. "See ya."

November 25, 1945
Sunday Morning

Sara spent the next two days wondering what Izzie wanted. Her mind traveled down a dozen different pathways. Each one returned to the same intersection of vagueness. By the time Sunday morning rolled around, she was weary of asking herself questions for which she could not fathom answers.

Kent left early Sunday morning, but not before he kissed her goodbye. She wanted to believe they had come to a compromise about her attending church both Sunday morning and Sunday night. She knew it was really no more than a stalemate.

After Sunday morning church services, Sara made a turkey sandwich for her lunch, and then went to sit in the living room waiting for Izzie to put in an appearance.

The minutes ticked by. One fifteen. One twenty. Sara's mind hopped back to the scene in Martha's kitchen on Thanksgiving Day. *I wasn't imagining things. Kent bears a marked resemblance to Mrs. Mac.* It has to be more than a coincidence. Can't Martha and Lester see what is right before their eyes? Maybe they have seen it. Maybe...

A knock sounded on the front door. Izzie was here.

Chapter Thirty

November 25, 1945
Sunday Afternoon

Sara asked Izzie inside, invited her to sit on the couch, and then took a seat beside her. There seemed no point in postponing asking the reason for her visit. "I'm glad you're here. How can I help you?"

"I'm getting married New Year's Eve. I'm hoping you will—"

"Wait a minute." Sara held up one hand. "When did this happen? Who is the boy? When did you meet him and where? Fill me in on the details."

"He's not a boy. He's a man. He will graduate from the Mount Zion Seminary next May. After that he will be a missionary. We are going to Africa in September."

"But you're so young." A dozen unmanageable thoughts crowded into Sara's mind. "What does your mother say?"

"She says she'd stop me if she could." Izzie lowered her eyes and bit her bottom lip. "She thinks religion is foolishness. That's why I've come to you. Mama refuses to have anything to do with me marrying a preacher-man."

Sara would love to help her friend, but first she had to ask one very important question. "How old are you, Izzie?"

"I'm nineteen. That's why Mama can't keep me from marrying Andrew." Izzie laid her hand on Sara's arm. "We could run away, but I want a nice wedding we can remember with pride. Please, Sara, will you help me? In a way you're responsible for me meeting Andrew. You introduced me to Pastor Frank who told me about Jesus. If you hadn't, I would never have gone to the First Missionary Church. That's where I met Andrew."

"Why did you choose that church?" The only First Missionary Church Sara knew about had a huge congregation and a minister known nationwide for his oratorical abilities and his numerous best-selling books.

"That's where Mrs. Mac goes, and it's near enough that we can walk there. Will you help me?"

"You know I will." Sara could foresee this occurrence having far–reaching complications. "Tell me how you met Andrew."

"He's my Sunday school teacher. Mrs. Mac introduced him to me." Izzie's face took on a dreamy expression. "When I told him I didn't understand much of what he was teaching, he offered to tutor me."

"What is Andrew's last name?" A red flag went up in Sara's mind. This young man could be what he claimed. On the other hand, he might be a wolf in sheep's clothing.

'His name is Andrew Joshua Faulkner."

"Is he related to Henry Faulkner?" Sara couldn't believe what she was hearing. Henry Faulkner was the much-revered pastor of the First Missionary Church.

"Reverend Faulkner is Andrew's daddy. He's going to assist Pastor Frank in our wedding ceremony."

It took a while for Sara to process all that Izzie had told her. When she finally did, she asked, "Are you telling me Reverend Faulkner approves of this marriage?"

"Why wouldn't he?" Izzie asked with innocent candor. "We love each other and we are both children of God."

"Reverend Faulkner is not going to perform the ceremony?"

"How could I let anyone but Pastor Frank perform my wedding ceremony?" Izzie asked with some indignation before she added, "He's the person who first told me about Jesus."

"I see your point." The distinguished Reverend Faulkner would be playing second fiddle to Pastor Frank, a dwarf who pastored an insignificant little church on the wrong side of town. God did move in mysterious ways.

"Will you make my wedding dress?" Izzie clapped her hands together. "I have the pattern. Will you help me shop for the material? Will you stand with me during the ceremony?"

"What about your sister"? Sara asked. "Wouldn't you rather have her as your maid of honor?"

"She's not eighteen yet and Mama refuses to let her even come to the wedding." Izzie frowned. "Sometimes Mama can be downright mean."

"I will be honored to stand with you." Sara wanted to agree with Izzie's assessment of her mother. Second thoughts made her reconsider and change the subject. "Who is going to give you away?"

"Mr. Holden, if he will. I haven't asked him yet because I haven't told Mrs. Holden I'm not coming back to work after December 15th. I need some time before my wedding, and Andrew doesn't want me to work after we are married."

When she could get her breath and collect her wits Sara asked, "You want *Lester* to give you away? Why him?"

"He is always nice to me and he takes my side when Mrs. Holden scolds me."

To Sara, that seemed a poor reason to ask someone to give you away. She was set to object and once more changed her mind. This was Izzie's wedding. If she wanted Lester to give her away, so be it. "You should ask him soon, don't you think?"

"I will, on December 8th, that's when I will tell Mrs. Holden I won't be back after December 15th."

"Don't you think you should tell her sooner?" Sara had no idea how Martha would react to such news. With Martha, one never knew.

"Mrs. Mac says December 8th is soon enough." Izzie snapped her fingers. "I just remembered. Mrs. Mac says she will come with me when I come to see you next Sunday. She wants to help with the wedding."

"I may have other plans for next Sunday." Izzie was taking an awful lot for granted.

"I never thought of that." Izzie frowned. "Do you?"

"No." An ache moved in around Sara's heart. How could she be so cruel? Izzie was a babe in Christ. Her mother had deserted her. Sara was the nearest thing she had to a friend, and at this moment, she was not being a very good friend. *I am a poor example for being Christ-like.* "I don't. I look forward to meeting with you and Mrs. Mac."

"Thank you." Izzie breathed a deep sigh of relief.

Sara wondered, what have I let myself in for?

November 26, 1945
Monday Evening

Sara waited until after dinner, when Kent was settled in his easy chair and she had picked up her sewing, to tell her husband about Izzie's coming wedding. "Your mother doesn't know yet. Please don't mention it to her before Izzie has time to tender her resignation."

"Mother already knows." Kent laid his paper aside. "She's happy for Izzie. And for herself."

"For herself? Who told her?" Sara laid her sewing aside. Why chance puncturing her finger with a needle a second time?

"Mother became suspicious of something Izzie said about having a secret." Kent shrugged. "You know Mother, she gave Izzie the third degree and Izzie told her."

"I'm glad she's pleased. Did she tell you Izzie wants Lester to give her away?"

"Yes, she did, and she wasn't pleased at first." Kent chuckled. "She was fit to be tied until she learned who the bridegroom is. When Mother saw the possibility of having near-kinship and definite friendship with the illustrious Faulkner family, she decided to not only to see to it that Farther gave Izzie away, but offered to buy Izzie's wedding gown."

Sara said a silent *Thank you, Jesus.*

"I have a surprise for you." Kent moved from his chair and sat on the couch beside Sara.

"What is it?" As if he hadn't already surprised her.

"I talked on the telephone to your family today." He smiled that killer-smile that always sent her heart racing. "Mama and Grandma are coming to spend Christmas with us."

"That's wonderful." She threw her arms around his neck. Mama and Grandma were coming to spend some time with her. Her heart sang and then she remembered. "What about James, and Junior, and Peggy Sue?"

"I invited them. James doesn't think it wise for Peggy Sue to make the trip since she's seven months pregnant. They will spend Christmas Day with Peggy Sue's family." He brushed her cheek with his lips, sending a tingle down her spine. "Mama and Grandma will be here December the 10th, and they won't leave to go back to the farm until the 2nd of next January. James thinks Mama needs to get away for a while. "

"You sent them bus tickets, didn't you?" She put her arms around his waist and squeezed tight. "You are the best husband in the world."

"You are only saying that because it's true." Kent laughed at his own droll humor and then kissed her deeply and passionately. The world around her faded like mist kissed by sunlight. Her only reality was this man and this moment.

Chapter Thirty-One

December 10, 1945
Monday Morning

Time hurried by, each day stepping on the heels of the last as they sped past. Soon December 10th arrived. Mama and Grandma would arrive this afternoon.

The last several days had been busy ones, too busy for Sara to dwell on the one question that was uppermost in her mind, Kent's resemblance to Mrs. Mac.

As November faded into December, Sara, Izzie, and Mrs. Mac worked out the details of Izzie's wedding and shopped for a wedding dress at the very exclusive dress shop Martha selected. Each time Izzie voiced concern about the amount of money Martha was spending, Mrs. Mac waved her objection aside. "She wouldn't have it any other way. How else could she hobnob with the likes of Reverend Faulkner and his wife?"

The reception would be in the recreation room of the First Missionary Church. When Martha heard that news, she appointed herself in charge of the entire affair. She hired a decorator and ordered an elaborate cake. Working out the details required that she confer often with Reverend Faulkner and his wife. Sara was amazed at the way she managed to worm herself into the good graces of the Faulkners in so short a time.

Sara was preparing the spare bedroom for Mama and Grandma when someone knocked on the front door. She hurried to the living room. Before she could reach her destination, two more loud raps.

"I'm coming, hang on." She picked up her pace. Seconds later she swung open the door.

Mama, Grandma, and Kent stood on the other side. "I thought—you're early." She opened the door.

Mama, Kent, and Grandma shouted in unison, "Surprise."

"I'll get the bags." Kent turned in the direction of his car.

"I'm so glad to see you." Sara hugged Mama and Grandma before hugging both of them again.

"Everything looks nice." Grandma's gaze swept around the room. "Kent has been telling us how you transformed this place from a house into a home."

"You should see the rest of the place." Kent came through the front door loaded down with bags and suitcases. "One more load, ladies, and you're all moved in."

"I was wrong about your husband. I've been wrong about so many things." Mama sat on the couch as Grandma followed Kent into the spare bedroom, chatting a mile a minute as she went.

"I am glad you and Grandma are getting the chance to know him better." For the first time since they had come into the room, Sara really looked at her mama. She had lost weight. The lines in her face had deepened. The streaks of gray in her hair were broader and more pronounced. She was grieving herself right into old age. "Would you like to see your bedroom?"

"I will see it soon enough." Mama pointed toward Kent's easy chair. "Sit down. James and Peggy Sue send their love."

Kent and Grandma came back into the room, and then Kent went for the rest of the bags.

"Kent showed me both bedrooms, and the bath. Imagine, a bathtub and a shower." Grandma sat on the couch beside Mama. "You did a good job decorating your little house, Sara. I'm proud of you."

"Thank you, Grandma." Sara sat in the easy chair. She was pleased that Kent had complimented her. Grandma's approval was even more gratifying. Grandma didn't hand out praises unless she meant every word she said, and she had no problem criticizing if she thought it was deserved. Sara thanked God for this special moment of happiness.

The days passed in pleasant repetition. Mama and Grandma helped Sara in the kitchen. Always before she had been their assistant. When she mentioned that fact, Grandma said, "It's your kitchen. You have the final word. That's the way it's supposed to be. A woman's kitchen is her domain."

The three of them had long discussions about the farm, and reminisced about memories they shared. Mama bragged about James, what a good farmer he was, and what a fine father he was to Junior. "I can hardly wait to see him with a child of his own." Grandma talked about her garden and how this year she had a bumper crop. Sara related how she came to find her house and how she shopped for furniture. She couldn't help doing some bragging of her own about the bargains she found. The one missing subject in their sharing was any mention of Daddy. Each time his name was brought up, Mama skillfully steered the talk in another direction.

In the afternoons, they donned their sweaters and took walks around the neighborhood. This gave Sara the opportunity to introduce her visitors to her neighbors. Both Grandma and Mama were impressed by how friendly everyone was. Grandma said they were just like people at home and Mama agreed.

When they arrived back at the house on Friday afternoon, Grandma declared she was "tuckered out," and went to her bedroom for a nap.

This was the opportunity Sara had waited for. She made a fresh pot of coffee and insisted Mama sit down and enjoy a cup. Then she began preparing supper. "I can help," Mama offered.

"I don't need help. I do need to talk to you." Sara sat a cup on the table.

Mama sat down. The expression on her face was one of wary expectation.

Sara poured coffee into the cup, and set out cream and saccharine. "What are we having tonight?" Mama poured cream into her coffee. "Are you sure I can't help?"

"Pork chops, creamed potatoes, and a vegetable salad." Sara peeled potatoes and put them in a pan. "Why won't you talk about Daddy?"

"There is nothing to say. He's dead. I am responsible for that." Mama took a sip of coffee and frowned. "I can make the salad."

"You are not—" Sara stopped. She could argue until doomsday and Mama would not be persuaded. "Have you asked God to forgive you?"

"I killed my husband. God won't forgive me for that."

"You always taught me God would forgive anything except the sin of disbelief in His Son." Sara was being harsh, but it was in the pursuit of kindness.

"I should have nailed the door shut." Tears fell into Mama's coffee. "Why didn't I?"

"Because God was ready to take Daddy home." Sara laid her knife and her potato on the cabinet counter, sat in the chair next to Mama, and scooted it close. "Answer one question for me. If you could call him back, and he would be just the way he was when he went, would you?"

Mama's answer was tomb-like silence.

"Answer me, Mama. Tell me, would you?" Sara took both her mother's hands in her own. "Would you call him back to be like he was when he left?"

"No." Mama's anguished whisper could barely be heard.

"You don't feel guilty because Daddy is dead. You feel guilty because you don't wish him back. Stop it, Mama. Daddy is better off in heaven. Don't question God."

Dora broke into an outburst of tears.

"It's all right, Mama." Sara held her mother in her arms. "It's all right."

"Weeping, at last." Grandma stood in the doorway. "She hasn't shed a tear since God took your daddy home."

Chapter Thirty-Two

December 16, 1945
Sunday Morning

As usual, Kent left the house early Sunday morning. He kissed Sara goodbye at the front door. He was completely silent about where he was going or when he would return. Would she ever understand him?

Sara was in the kitchen putting the finishing touches on her Sunday dinner when Mama and Grandma came into the room. She called out a cheery, "Good morning, sleepy heads."

"I never slept so late before in all my life." Mama stretched and yawned.

"I wake up at five every morning." Grandma filled two cups with coffee and set them on the table. "Then I turn over and go right back to sleep."

"I am glad you are both getting a good rest." Sara untied her apron and hung it on a hook. "I'm going to get dressed for church. Make yourselves at home."

She hurried to her bedroom. Sooner or later her mother or her grandmother, or both, would ask where Kent was. Sara preferred it to be later.

She was both pleased and proud to take Mama and Grandma to church with her. The service was, as always, spiritually uplifting. The congregation welcomed her guests. Afterward, they lingered, talking and visiting until Sara insisted they should get home. "Izzie and Mrs. Mac will be arriving soon."

As they walked around the church toward home, Grandma asked the question Sara knew was coming. "Where is Kent? Why wasn't he at church?"

"Kent doesn't attend church." Sara recalled what a problem she created by not being straightforward about her marriage to Kent in the beginning. It was a lesson well-learned.

"Why not?" Grandma asked.

Sara would be glad to answer that question, if she knew what the answer was. "I don't know. Let's get home and have dinner."

December 16, 1945

Sunday Afternoon

Izzie's reunion with Mama and Grandma was pleasant.

Sara made introductions. "Mama, this is my friend, Mrs. Mac. Mrs. Mac, meet my Mama, Dora." The two shook hands and exchanged pleasantries. "This," said Sara, with a touch of pride in her voice, "Is my Grandma Belle."

Grandma smiled and nodded. "I'm pleased to meet you, Mrs. Mac.

Soon the four were chatting like old friends. Mrs. Mac was telling of the groom's cake she planned to make when a strange car pulled into the driveway.

"Were you expecting someone?" Sara asked Izzie.

Before Izzie could answer, Martha got out of the back seat of the car and came up the walk toward the front door.

Anxiety cramped into Sara's stomach. "What could *she* possibly want?"

"I have no idea," Mrs. Mac answered. "But I'm sure we are about to find out."

Sara answered the knock on the door as the car drove away.

"Kent thinks I should come over and meet your mother and grandmother." Without waiting for an invitation, Martha stepped around Sara and swept into the room.

"Kent suggested you come here?" Mrs. Mac's voice carried enough venom to stop Martha in her tracks.

Sara took command of the situation and made introductions. "Mama, Grandma, this is Kent's mother, Mrs. Holden." She recalled the quarrel Martha and Mrs. Mac had because Izzie told Martha how Sara learned of this house. They were headed in that direction again. She had to stop them, but how?

"Mrs. Holden, indeed." Martha sat on the couch beside Grandma. "You must call me Martha. We are family, after all." She aimed a wicked glare in Mrs. Mac's direction. "At least most of us are."

"My name's Belle." Grandma doubled her fist and pointed her thumb in Mama's direction. "My daughter is Dora." She asked Mrs. Mac, "What's your Christian name, honey?"

"Theresa," Mrs. Mac responded immediately, and with dignity. "But my friends call me Tessie."

"Tessie it is." Grandma snapped her fingers. "Now, can we get back to the business of planning this coming wedding?"

"I hardly think that is appropriate, considering the circumstances." Martha had a look of fierce determination on her face.

"You're included, too." Grandma patted Martha's arm. "Seeing as how you have a lot of time and money invested in the reception and your husband is giving the bride away." She turned to Dora. "What do you think, dear?"

Sara scrunched down on her chair. *This is going to be a disaster.*

"Maybe we should get Izzie's opinion about what is appropriate," Dora said, and then added, "It's her wedding."

"You miss my point." Martha was not about to let go. "Izzie and Mrs. Mac are my employees. It is inappropriate for them to call me by my given name."

"I see we are of two minds about this," Grandma said, and then asked, "What should we do?"

A dark cloud of silence fell over the room and lingered.

"Let's talk to God. I never had a problem that was too big to pray through." Grandma bowed her head. "Father God, thank you for the privilege of approaching Your Throne of Grace through our Lord Jesus. Speak to our hearts now. Show each one us what You would have us do about our name calling dilemma. I ask this prayer in the name of my precious Lord Jesus. Amen."

"Amen," Sara echoed. Grandma's sweet prayer left her humbled and shamed by her own thoughts and actions.

"If Mrs. Holden prefers we call her Mrs. Holden, that's all right with me." Mrs. Mac brushed at a tear. "Jesus was humble enough to wash His disciples' feet. Why should I quibble about a name?"

Izzie nodded her agreement. "Both Mrs. Mac and I will call you Mrs. Holden, Mrs. Holden."

"I had no idea I was coming to a gathering of religious fanatics." Martha stood and grabbed her handbag. "I thought you were planning a wedding, not holding a prayer meeting."

"Does this mean Mr. Holden won't give me away?" Izzie wrung her hands and looked distressed. "If he can't, I have to call Reverend Faulkner right now. He said if there was any change of plans I should let him know immediately." She moved toward the telephone.

"No, don't." The mention of Reverend Faulkner's name had a quelling effect on Martha. She sat back down. "Now that this name business is settled. Of course, Lester will give you away."

"Let's get on with our plans." Dora looked at her daughter and shrugged. That look and shrug said more than a thousand words could have expressed.

Discussion began again, this time with a little less warmth. More than once, Sara thanked God for her grandmother's presence. Each time Martha became pushy or demanding about some disagreed upon subject, Grandma suggested they pray about it. Martha either gave in or shut up.

As the meeting progressed, Sara was struck by a revelation. She seldom included God in her plans or asked His help in making decisions. Swift on the heels of that revelation came another disclosure. Grandma was not doing this to manipulate Martha. She was sincerely including God in her plans and honestly asking for His help in making decisions.

Sara tried to relax as the conversation continued to move along smoothly. She didn't draw an easy breath until after Martha's driver returned to take her home. Izzie and Mrs. Mac left shortly after.

As they walked down the sidewalk returning from seeing Mrs. Mac and Izzy to the bus stop, Grandma sighed and shook her head. "I'm beginning to see why Kent doesn't go to church."

"It's an impossible situation." Sara drew a long breath.

"We all have a thorn in our flesh," Mama said.

"Maybe Martha is Sara's," Grandma added.

So much for sympathy from these two. They went inside the house and Sara immediately headed toward the kitchen. "Supper is leftovers." Mama followed her. "Now that we have a handle on Izzie's wedding plans, we should start planning for Christmas."

Grandma followed Mama. "I'm thinking of making a fruit cake. I still have time and that recipe that uses syrup for sweetener."

Chapter Thirty-Three

December 19, 1945
Wednesday Afternoon

Sara waited for the chance to talk to her mother alone. It was a long time coming. Friday afternoon Grandma decided to take a nap. Sara took advantage of the opportunity and guided Mama into the kitchen on the pretense of showing her a new recipe.

"A recipe, huh?" Mama sat at the table and gazed at her daughter with a questioning look in her eyes. "Sit down, Sara, and tell me what you really brought me in here to say."

"Am I that transparent?" Sara sat across from her mother.

"I'm your mama. What's bothering you, Sweetie?"

"Do you see a resemblance between Kent and Mrs. Mac?" Before the words escaped her mouth, she was sorry for having said them. Was she borrowing trouble? As if she didn't have problems enough already.

"I hadn't noticed it." Mama's face creased into a frown. "Why do you ask?"

"No reason." Relief made Sara sigh.

"Now that you mention it. I do see some resemblance. Not a big one, mind you, but if you look expecting, it's there." Mama splayed her hand across her throat. "Sara." Her voice was high pitched and unsteady. "What are you trying to tell me?"

"Should I pursue this further? Kent is adopted. Is there the slightest chance Mrs. Mac could be related to him? I don't want to stir up trouble and find I was mistaken. I do need to know. Oh, how I need to know."

"Why?" Mama asked, and then tagged her first question with yet another query. "Does it make a difference to you?"

"No." Sara was emphatic. "Never, but it does to him. He's bothered by not knowing who he *really* is. He never wants to have any children. Never Mama, *never*." The tears she swore she wouldn't shed surfaced and slid down her cheeks.

"Oh, Sara, darling, have you prayed about this?"

"I've asked God at least a hundred times to change Kent's mind. Why doesn't He answer my prayers?" Sara wiped her eyes on her the hem of her dress.

"Have you ever prayed that God's will be done?" Mama scooted her chair around the table to sit near Sara. "Have you ever prayed, 'God show me the way, and I'll follow'?"

She hadn't. Sara had blithely assumed because she wanted a family, God would give her one.

From what seemed a long way off, Mama's voice called, "Sara, have you?"

"What should I do?" Sara laid her head on her mother's shoulder.

"You're asking the wrong person." Mama kissed her cheek. "That is between you and God. Do you want to pray about it now?"

Sara's throat was too full to speak. She nodded, signaling she did, and then bowed her head.

Mama followed suit, and spoke in a hushed voice, "Dear heavenly Father, it seems the daughter you gave into my keeping has problems that only You can solve. Should she go poking around in the past? Should she demand a show-down with Kent over the question of having children? Help her now to receive some answer from You."

Sara spoke to her heavenly Father, "Not my will, God, but thine." Help me to step out on faith and follow Your lead." She poured her heart out to her Lord Jesus. As she spoke, a great burden lifted. She raised her head and smiled through her tears at her mother. The sweet peace of the Holy Spirit filled her soul. Things might get worse, before they got better, but she had her answer. She would bide her time, and when the opportunity presented itself, she knew what she must do.

December 19, 1945
Wednesday Evening

Late Wednesday afternoon a cold and unexpected norther blew across the city, rattling windows, and moving with force through the trees.

"I can't sell cars in weather like this." Kent came through the front door, bringing with him a gust of cold air.

Sara greeted him with a kiss and a hug. "It's an ill wind that blows no good. I'm glad you are home. Come into the kitchen. Supper will be ready soon."

"Where are your mama and your grandma?" Kent looked around the room.

"They went to the Wednesday afternoon Ladies' Bible study at the church. They will be home soon." She waved for Kent to sit down. "We are having leftover roast, green peas, and creamed potatoes for supper. Earlier today Mama made cookies using molasses for sweetener."

"That sounds good to me. I am going to miss Mama and Grandma when they go home. They are spoiling me with their desserts, but at the present, I'm glad we're alone. Can you sit down for a few minutes? I have something to tell you."

"Okay." A chill ran down Sara's backbone as she sat in a chair and folded her hands on the table. *Please, God, don't let it be bad news.*

"Father wants us, you, me, Mama, and Grandma, to have Christmas dinner with him and Mother."

Surely Martha didn't expect Izzie and Mrs. Mac to work on Christmas day. "I don't think Mama and Grandma would be comfortable having Christmas dinner in a restaurant, even an elegant one. Why don't they come here? We haven't shopped yet, and two more people—" Another, and more disturbing, thought crowded into her mind. "How does your mother feel about this?"

"The meal won't be in a restaurant. It will be at their home. Mrs. Mac has agreed to cook it. Mother is all for it."

"Are you sure? What about Mrs. Mac's Christmas? Doesn't she want to spend Christmas with her family?" Sara could hardly tell the husband she adored that she didn't fancy spending Christmas Day with his mother.

"Mrs. Mac doesn't have a family. Her husband died years ago, and her only son was killed in the war." Kent reached for her hand. "I suspect this was Mother's idea. I also suspect Mrs. Mac is receiving a huge bonus for her Christmas Day labors." He smiled at her and her heart melted. "What do you say, shall we go?"

Mama and Grandma came through the door, admitting another gust of cold air. "Go where?" Grandma asked.

"My parents have invited us to be their guests for Christmas dinner."

"That's wonderful," Grandma chortled. "It will give us all a chance to get better acquainted."

"Sara hasn't yet agreed to go." Kent stood. "We were discussing the matter. Come on into the kitchen. I will help Sara get dinner on the table."

"Of course, we will go." Mama levelled a long, narrowed glance in Sara's direction. "Won't we, daughter?"

"Yes, of course." Sara moved toward the stove. She had been betrayed by her own flesh and blood.

Chapter Thirty-Four

December 22, 1945
Saturday

The last few days had been joyful. On Thursday, Mama, Grandma, and Sara went shopping. They bought gifts for Kent, Martha, Lester, Izzie, and Mrs. Mac.

Kent came home early loaded with packages that he stored in a closet. That evening Grandma played her harmonica and they sang Christmas carols. Later, Kent told Sara that he couldn't remember when he had enjoyed an evening more.

Friday, Kent came home at noon, bringing with him a Christmas tree and decorations for it and the house. They set about to accomplish those tasks. Later they enjoyed homemade molasses cookies and coffee. A festive Christmas spirit permeated everything they did.

The one dark spot was when Mama recalled, with sadness, past Christmases, when Daddy cut a tree from the woods for them to decorate. "Those were such happy times." Mama wiped at a tear.

"Shame on you, Dora," Grandma chided. "You can't go back and relive the past, except in your memory. Be thankful for what you once had, but live in the now."

Kent smiled as he asked Grandma, "How did you get so wise?"

"Through experience," Grandma replied. "It teaches us hard lessons, and we learn, oh how we learn." She laughed. "Those are my words of wisdom for today. Let's have some more cookies and coffee."

Saturday morning Kent surprised Sara as he sat down to breakfast by telling her that he was taking the day off. "I have plans for today," he added, as he poured cream into his coffee.

"Does Lester know you won't be in your office today?" Sara set a platter of Spam and eggs and a pan of hot biscuits on the table. "Is he okay with you missing a day of work?"

Before she could say more, Mama and Grandma came through the kitchen door. Sara waved for them to sit down at the table and poured coffee for everyone before she sat across from Kent.

"Let's ask God's blessings on the food." Grandma bowed her head and prayed.

Kent raised his head with a surprised look on his handsome face. He didn't comment.

"We heard you two talking about a surprise." Mama stirred saccharine into her coffee. "Is it a secret or can we know?"

"It's my surprise." Kent forked a generous helping of Spam and eggs into his plate before sliding two biscuits in beside them. "Ladies. I am taking you to Lady Sylvia's Tea Room for lunch."

"I've never been to a tea room." Grandma clapped her hands together. "This is so exciting."

"How sweet of you, dear." Sara's joy was dampened by the thought that Martha might also be invited on this outing. "How thoughtful of you."

"What do you wear to a tea room?" Dora asked.

"Your best bib-and-tucker." Grandma pushed back her chair and made ready to stand. "I'm glad I brought my Sunday hat."

"Don't go yet." Kent held up one hand. "That's not all. After lunch the four of us are going to see *Christmas in Connecticut* at the Strand."

"The Strand?" Sara echoed. The Strand was the most expensive movie theater in the city. He had said the four of us. Thank heavens for that.

Mama was on her feet and Grandma was already to the door. Sara stood. "I have to decide what to wear." She stopped beside Kent's chair. "Thank you, my darling, for the most wonderful surprise I ever had." She kissed his cheek. Grandma's admonition sounded in her ears. *Be thankful for what you once had, but live in the now.*

The tea room was the epitome of elegance. The Victorian decor added an air of refinement. Mama held onto Sara's arm and whispered into her ear, "All this sophistication is intimidating." Grandma was having the time of her life. She told Kent, "I've never seen a finer place. I'm glad I wore my Sunday hat."

It would be difficult to determine who was happier with the surroundings, Grandma or Kent. Sara's nerves calmed when she saw the look of pleasure on Kent's face. If he was happy, she was happy.

They were shown to a choice table near a window. The waitress brought menus.

"What will you have, ladies?" Kent studied his menu.

"I'll have the victory luncheon." Grandma looked over her glasses toward Kent. "If that's all right with you. Ninety–five cents seems a heap of money to pay for one meal, but you get a lot of food, even dessert."

"Have what you want," Kent told her. "This is one of my Christmas gifts to you." Mama and Sara ordered the victory luncheon also.

Sara tasted her soup. It was delicious. She watched as Grandma charmed her husband with her wit and her honest observations about the tea room's patrons. Grandma was a flirt. If she was fifty years younger, Sara would be jealous. Since that wasn't the case, she was pleased that Kent found her grandmother so fascinating.

On the way home, Grandma and Mama discussed the movie, dissecting each scene and imputing motives to every character.

Over supper, Mama said this was a day she would long remember. "Not many perfect days come along. When I have one, I store it in my memory and take it out to live again when I feel sad or discouraged."

Kent and Sara went to bed early. Sara was anxious to be in her husband's arms. He had given her a perfect day. She would give him a perfect night.

They came together in a fiery storm of lovemaking. Later as Sara lay in his arms, satisfied and fulfilled, she whispered to him how much she loved him.

"I love you too, sweet Sara." He pulled her closer to him.

"Every day, I thank God for letting me find such a wonderful man as you."

"Never say that again." Kent leaped from the bed. His feet hit the floor with a thud. He made long strides toward the bathroom.

All the magic of the day, all the enchantment of the night, drained from Sara, leaving her feeling flat and empty. What did she do? What did she say that upset him? She curled into a fetal position, buried her head in her pillow, and wept.

Chapter Thirty-Five

December 23, 1945
Sunday Morning

"I'm leaving now." Kent stood at the door with his hat in his hand and his jacket over his arm. "Before I go let me apologize for my outburst last night."

"What did I say that upset you so?" Sara came from the couch to stand before him. All through breakfast she had waited for him to comment on his sudden explosion. He didn't. She debated with herself about mentioning it to him and decided to wait until some more convenient time. "Maybe I should apologize to you, too."

"Nonsense." He leaned over and kissed her cheek. "It's me, not you."

"Come back and sit down. We can talk about it."

"Some other time." He waved her request aside. "I am going to help Father with some bookwork and visit Mother. Tell Mama and Grandma I will see them at dinner." He was through the door and gone before Sara could object.

She went back to the kitchen and sat down as thoughts of last night's events played through her mind. She didn't know what had upset him. She did know that things couldn't go on as they were.

She was nursing a cold cup of coffee and chasing opposing thoughts around in her head when Mama and Grandma came through the door dressed for church. "You two are getting to be real sleepyheads. Sit down. Breakfast is ready." Sara hurried to the oven, retrieved a freshly-baked honey coffee cake, and set it on the table.

"I see from the amount of coffee cake left that you and Kent have had breakfast." Grandma helped herself to a generous slice. "Where is that man, anyway?"

"Don't be so nosy," Mama scolded. "Where Kent is doesn't concern you."

"He went to help his Father with bookwork and to visit his mother." Thank goodness that, at last, she had an answer to that question.

"We have had such a wonderful visit." Mama pointed her fork in Sara's direction. "You and Kent have showed us such hospitality."

"We love having you here."

"I know, and appreciate that, still sometimes I think we should go home early." Mama took a swift sup of coffee. "I feel guilty about leaving James and Peggy Sue with all that work for so long, but we can't miss Izzie's wedding."

"We certainly can't," Grandma said over a big bite of coffee cake. "Izzie is such a sweet girl and she's dedicated her life to carrying the Gospel of Christ to the lost souls in Africa."

"Don't forget about all the friends we have made here." Mama pushed the plate from her. "Mrs. Mac and all the ladies at church. I have the addresses of at least six people I will be writing to." She waved her hands in Sara's direction. "Go and get ready for church. Grandma and I will do the dishes and straighten the kitchen. Give me your apron."

December 23, 1945
Sunday Afternoon

Izzie and Mrs. Mac arrived early in the afternoon, bringing with them gifts and food. The plans for the wedding were set, but the five women had decided to have a little Christmas party to celebrate their friendship.

Grandma was so taken with her recent visit to a tea room that she bought a dainty little teapot and six matching cups and saucers. She had the table laid before Izzie and Mrs. Mac arrived.

Izzie was as excited as a child. "I had a little tea set once when I was a girl. I wonder where it is now."

They drank tea and enjoyed Mama's scrumptious sandwiches and Mrs. Mac's delicious sugar-free pastries.

Sara's enjoyment was diminished by the fear that Martha night decide to call once more, uninvited, and crash their party. As time passed, that fear subsided, and she relaxed.

The gifts they exchanged were inexpensive and homemade. Izzie gave each of the other women two potholders and two tea towels. She announced, with pride, that she made them herself. "I'm learning how to use a sewing machine. I will have to make most of what we wear when we get to Africa."

Mrs. Mac gave little files of index cards with ten of her favorite recipes printed on them. "I have had some of these recipes for years. They are all fool-proof if you follow the directions."

Mama gave each of the others a split bonnet. "These are great to wear when you go outside in the spring and summer, but be sure to take the slats out before you wash them."

Sara made aprons for the others. She used the leftover material she had after making her curtains and trimmed them with contrasting bias tape.

Grandma gave hemstitched linen handkerchiefs for gifts. "How," Mrs. Mac wondered aloud, "did you make four hand-stitched handkerchiefs so fast?"

"I didn't. I make these all year round."

"She buys little remnants of linen every time she goes to town." Sara pressed her handkerchief to her face. "These get softer each time they are washed."

All too soon the afternoon was over and Izzie and Mrs. Mac left to catch their bus home.

Chapter Thirty-Six

December 25, 1945
Tuesday Morning

Sara woke early. This was a day she had looked forward to with both anxiety and anticipation. She would hope for the best and prepare for the worst. She reached to touch Kent. He was not there.

"Good morning," he called from the doorway. "Merry Christmas. Rise and shine. Breakfast is ready."

"You made breakfast?" Sara sat on the side of the bed.

"I made coffee." He smiled that smile that never failed to set her pulse racing. "I bought breakfast. Hot yeast buns from the neighborhood bakery."

Mama and Grandma joined them for breakfast. They were in a festive mood. wishing each other Merry Christmas and looking forward to the coming day.

Kent was in a joyous mood, also. He teased Mama and Grandma by saying he made the buns they were eating.

They were not fooled. "These," Mama said, after she wiped her mouth with a paper napkin, "were made by a pro."

They were all in such high spirits. Sara wasn't. She couldn't shake a feeling of an impending disaster.

Later they gathered around the Christmas tree and exchanged gifts. Sara tried to push her uneasiness aside. It wouldn't go away.

Mama gave Sara a cookbook, Kent two large tins of his favorite tobacco, and Grandma several skeins of wool yarn for knitting.

Grandma gave Sara a pair of scissors with the admonition that she should take care of them. "They are for cutting material only. Use your old scissors when you cut paper." She gave Kent a beautiful hand knitted sweater. "I made James one like it, except his is blue and yours is brown." She gave Mama enough yard goods to make two dresses. "I got two shades of your favorite color, green."

Sara was anxious to pass her gifts to their owners. She gave Mama and Grandma soft woolen shawls and Kent a briar pipe.

"This is the best Christmas ever." Kent was as excited as a little boy. He gave Mama a gold cross on an exquisite chain, Grandma a cameo broach, and Sara a tiny wrist watch.

"You shouldn't have spent so much money." Grandma pinned her broach to the neck of her dress. "But since you did, you chose the perfect gift. Thank you."

It would be difficult to judge who was more pleased with that gift, Grandma or Kent.

"This is lovely," Mama said, as Sara fastened her cross around her neck.

"I thought you would like it." Kent beamed with pride.

"Fasten my watch on my wrist." Sara extended her arm in Kent's direction.

"Do you like it?" he asked as he secured the clasp.

"I love it." Sara held her arm out for all to see. "I never had a watch before."

"I never had a Christmas like this before." Kent tamped tobacco into his pipe.

"All Christmases should be festive and happy." Sara looked at her loved ones gathered around her and felt a warm glow. "We are celebrating the birth of baby Jesus."

"Excuse me." Kent jumped from his chair and hurried from the room.

"What happened to him?" Mama sent a questioning gaze in Sara's direction

"I don't know," Sara answered. She was going to make it her business to find out. Sara packed her gifts for Martha and Lester into a basket that was already bulging with several kinds of goodies she had made for the occasion, three dozen of Mama's decorated molasses cookies and Grandma's fruitcake. "Is everyone ready to go? Martha says dinner will be served at two o'clock and it's almost one now."

The four of them loaded their treats and got into Kent's yellow Oldsmobile. They sang *Jingle Bells* and *Deck the Halls* as they drove across town.

As they pulled into the driveway, Lester came through the front door. He wore a bright red shirt and a Santa Claus cap. "Merry Christmas, everyone. Ho, ho, ho."

The living room was beautifully decorated. A huge Christmas tree stood in one corner, adorned with red velvet bows and sparkling lights.

"Your home is beautiful." Mama put the gifts she had brought under the tree.

"It should be." Lester smiled as he looked around the room. "The bill I got from the decorator Martha hired to do it looked like the national debt. Everybody, put your gifts under the tree and have a seat. Martha will make her grand entrance soon and we can all have a peek at what Santa brought us."

Mama never had to speak to convey her thoughts to her daughter. The look she sent Sara's way said more than a thousand words could have relayed.

Martha swept into the room. She wore a long red velvet dress trimmed around the neck, the hem, and the three-quarter sleeves, with white fur. "Welcome, everyone, to our humble abode." She smiled in Sara's direction. "I am so happy, Sara dear, to have your mother and grandmother here to spend this special holiday with us."

"We thank you for your invitation," Sara replied. If Martha was hoping to impress Mama and Grandma with her hoity-toity ways, she was wasting her time.

"Let's open presents." Lester rubbed his hands together. "I want to see what Santa Claus brought me." He read the name on each gift and then gave it to the recipient before sitting down and tearing into his own packages.

Martha's gift to each of her female guests was a best-selling novel. She chose *The Egg and I* for Grandma. *The Ghost and Mrs. Muir* was her selection for Sara. She gave Mama a copy of *So Well Remembered*. "My friend Julia Price says a good book is always an appropriate gift," she said, with a casual wave of her hand. Julia Price was undoubtedly an important person in Martha's life. Sara failed to recognize the name. Martha soon remedied that. "Julia is a poetess of some note, you know."

"I didn't know." Grandma perused her book. "This looks interesting. Thank you very much, Mrs. Holden."

Oh, Grandma, please. It's Martha, not Mrs. Holden.

"Yes, Martha, these are lovely gifts." Mama stepped in to save the day. "We all thank you, very much."

"Ain't these spiffy?" Lester held up the knitted cap and gloves from Grandma and the knitted scarf and matching hat from Mama. "Thank you, ladies." He laid them aside and held up his gift from Sara and Kent, a warm, fleecy bathrobe. "This is what I call classy. I bet Sara picked it out."

"She did, indeed." Kent chuckled. "Are you saying I have no class?"

"Sometimes you do. You chose Sara."

"You chose Mother. That speaks well for both of us." Kent's chuckle blossomed into a smile.

"Open your gift from me, Kent," Martha's voice raised to be heard above their conversation.

Kent lifted the wrappings from a beautiful cashmere cardigan. His breath caught in his throat. "It's beautiful. Thank you, Mother and Father."

"Don't thank your father. He had nothing to do with the purchase of that gift. The sweater is from me." Martha's mouth drew into a thin line.

"Kent knows that." Lester was not visibly upset by Martha's unpleasant remark. "I gave him his Christmas gift last week. Before you start asking questions, I gave him a bonus. Open your presents."

Martha, unpredictable as always, didn't argue, but opened a present. It was a long lovely strand of pearls from Lester. She held it up for all to see.

"They're the real thing," Lester boasted. "Yes, siree, the genuine real thing."

"I must wear these to Agatha's New Year's soiree." Martha wrapped the strand around her neck. Their luster shone with a muted glow against the red of her velvet dress.

"They're beautiful," Sara exclaimed.

Mama and Grandma agreed.

"I'm afraid our gifts to you," Mama said, as Martha undid the package from Grandma, "will pale by comparison to those lovely pearls."

"Nonsense." Martha lifted Grandma's hand knitted scarf for all to see. "This is very pretty." She was also pleased with Mama's hand knitted hat and gloves. She even voiced approval of the shawl from Sara and Kent. "I will put my gifts away and then we will go into dinner." She stood.

"Hold your horses." Lester stood. "I got one more gift to give. Excuse me."

"So do I." Kent reached into his shirt pocket and took out a small box. "It's for you, Mother." He came across the room.

"For me?" Martha laid her hand to the base of her throat. "Kent, you never gave me a gift before."

"Maybe it's time I did." He opened the box to reveal a ring with a pearl setting surrounded by four small diamonds. "This will match your necklace."

"It's beautiful." Martha slipped the ring on the third finger of her right hand. Tears stood in her eyes. "Thank you, son. I will treasure it always."

She gathered her gifts and left the room.

Martha shedding tears over a gift? That had to be a first.

Lester returned carrying a box that measured approximately ten inches by seven inches. "This is my gift to my daughter-in-law." He gave the box to Sara.

Surprise left her speechless.

"Open it, daughter." Mama's soft command brought Sara back to the present.

"Yes. Do." Kent came to stand on one side of her chair. "Father, you're the sneaky one. When did you buy this?"

Sara lifted the box lid to reveal a beautiful Scofield Bible. She swallowed and found her voice. "It's like the one Moses preaches from, only finer."

"It's the finest there is." Lester hunkered down on the other side of Sara's chair. "The cover is seal skin and it's sewed with genuine silk thread. Look down here." He pointed. "There's your name in red letters. It says *Sara Holden.*"

"I've wanted a Scofield Bible all of my life." The usually unflappable Grandma was impressed.

"It's top of the line," Lester bragged. "It has a concordance and thumb indexes. There's a ribbon book marker, every word Jesus spoke is in red, and the pages are edged in gold."

"It's beautiful. Thank you so much." Sara turned to speak to her husband. He was nowhere in sight.

"Where did that boy get off to?" Lester stood.

"Is anyone interested in Christmas dinner?" Martha appeared from nowhere.

"Yes indeed, we are." Mama, ever the peacemaker, led the way into the dining room.

Chapter Thirty-Seven

December 25, 1945
Tuesday Afternoon

Sara was relieved to see Kent standing behind a dining room chair. She opened her mouth to ask why he disappeared so suddenly. The stricken look on his face and the tight grip he had on his chair back stopped her. She sat in the chair next to him and gave him a reassuring smile.

Martha directed Mama and Grandma to sit across from Kent and Sara. She sat at the end of the table and nodded to Lester. "Sit down."

Lester obeyed and sat in the chair at the head of the table.

Grandma bowed her head and closed her eyes. The room became as silent as a mausoleum. She looked up and opened her eyes. "Lester, ask God to bless the food."

"Me?" Lester looked as though someone had belted him in the midsection. "I don't—that is—" His face was beet red.

"Yes. You are the head of this house, or aren't you?"

"We seldom say grace before meals." Martha helped herself to a large portion of sliced turkey breast.

"I always say grace." Grandma bowed her head and moved her lips in silent prayer.

Kent twisted in his chair.

"What's wrong, son?" The look on Lester's face was one of genuine concern.

That look triggered the memory of something Martha said when Sara first asked if Kent was adopted. *"Lester took me to see him. I said, then and there, 'I'm going to adopt this little boy' and I did."*

Lester must know about Kent's birth parents. Why had it taken her so long to see what was in plain sight all the time?

The food was delicious. The conversation was stilted and contrived.

Mama tried to keep dialogue going by telling cute stories about Junior and talking about James and Peggy Sue's expected baby. "Even Junior has begun to ask when his new brother or sister will get here."

"I have a headache, Mother." Kent stood and pressed his hand to his forehead." Where can I find some aspirin?"

"In the bathroom off the foyer."

"I'll get them." Lester jumped to his feet. "You keep your seat and finish your dinner. Mrs. Mac will come back and think we didn't like her cooking."

"Where is Mrs. Mac?" Grandma asked as Kent went toward the bathroom and Lester followed him.

Sara silently prayed. God, please put skid chains on Grandma's tongue.

"How would I know?" Martha raised an eyebrow. "I don't keep up with the comings and goings of the hired help."

Before Grandma could reply, Lester reentered the room.

"Where is Kent?" Sara stood, and rushed toward her father-in-law.

"I sent him upstairs to rest." Lester pointed over his shoulder with his thumb.

"Where upstairs?" Sara headed for the stairway.

"In his old quarters."

""Be a little more specific." Sara paused halfway up the landing.

"Where you and him stayed when you were here." Lester followed her. "Wait a minute. I need to talk to you."

Sara didn't slow her pace. This was so unlike Kent.

"Slow down." Lester caught up to her, puffing and out of breath. "Do you want me to have a heart attack?" He paused, held onto the banister with one hand, put the other one on his knee, and breathed deeply.

Sara reached the second-floor landing and stopped.

Once again Lester caught up to her. "Thank you."

"Sit down." Sara dropped to the first step that led to the third floor and patted the space beside her.

"Give me a moment." Lester sat beside her. He perspired profusely, and labored to catch his breath.

"Take your time." The last thing she needed now was for Lester to have a heart attack. "Are you all right?"

"Don't worry about me. I'm a tough old bird. Tell me what is wrong with my son."

"Your son?" Maybe this is the opportunity she had been waiting for. "I thought Kent was adopted."

"How I got Kent makes no difference. He's *my* son."

"How *did* you get Kent?" Sara leveled a penetrating gaze in Lester's direction.

"I want to know what is troubling Kent." Lester met her gaze with a stare of his own. "If you know, tell me."

Kent stood on the second riser above them. "I have a headache and you would think I had been stricken with some fatal disease." He spoke to his wife, "Sara, get Grandma and Mama and all your things. We're going home."

"Folks don't have headaches without some reason." Lester stood and faced Kent.

"Go." Kent nodded in Sara's direction. "I will be down in a few minutes."

Sara scooted back down the stairs with the sound of disagreeing voices following her.

The voices above her were soon replaced by those coming from the dining room.

She entered the room in time to catch the tail-end of Grandma's comment. "Martha Holden, you are a snob." She had jumped out of the frying pan and landed smack-dab in the fire.

"How is Kent feeling?" Martha shifted her gaze from Grandma to Sara.

"He wants to go home. He says we should get our things together."

"Sit down and finish your dinner first." Martha pointed to the chair Sara had previously vacated."

Sara sat.

"I owe you an apology." Grandma extended one hand in Martha's direction. "I shouldn't have called you a snob. It was not the Christian thing to do. Will you forgive me?"

"I will," Martha replied, very much on her dignity, "but only because I have a forgiving spirit."

"That's my girl." Lester came through the door with Kent in tow. "My boy has decided to stay a while longer and do justice to this sumptuous dinner."

"Are you sure?" Sara's voice was heavy with anxiety.

"I'm sure. Father and I had a talk. I feel much better now." Kent pulled out the chair beside his wife and sat down.

This was going to be a long afternoon. Sara took a quick sip of water to ease the dryness in her throat.

Chapter Thirty-Eight

December 31, 1945
Monday Afternoon

Sara stood in the crowded ante room behind the sanctuary of the First Missionary Church and waited for the signal to march down the center aisle. The room was filled to capacity with participants in the ceremony, and Martha, of course.

"I'm so nervous." Izzie clung to Lester's arm. She was radiant in a white satin wedding dress with a scoop neckline. Delicate lace appliques decorated the neckline and ran down the long sleeves. Her waist-length veil was fastened to her head with a lovely wreath of yellow rosebuds.

"Don't you worry none, little girl." Lester patted her hand. "Everything is going to be just fine."

In the sanctuary, two of Andrew's nieces lit the two tall candles that stood on either side of the podium as ushers set out folding chairs behind the last pews for late-arriving guests to sit in.

A lump rose in Sara's throat. She could have had a wedding such as this. She shouldn't complain. She loved her husband and he loved her. They would work out their problems.

She had tried several times since Christmas Day to talk to Kent about his headache episode. Each time she broached the subject, his reply was the same. "I had a headache. Don't make a federal case out of it." Sara made herself a promise. *After Izzie's wedding, Kent and I are going to have a conversation about his strange behavioral episodes, even if I have to tie him in a chair.*

That day had arrived. During the next hour Izzie would become Mrs. Andrew Faulkner.

"Everybody in line." Martha stood at the anteroom door. She had taken over the management of the wedding. Her sharp commands and demanding ways were tempered by the fact that Gladys Faulkner, Andrew's mother, was always near, hovering like a mother hen, and making sweetly worded suggestions and comments.

The organist struck a chord. The processional music began.

"An usher is seating Andrew's grandmother. The ministers, the groom, and the best man have entered." Martha straightened the little ring-bearer's tie. "Sara, you go first, then you two." She led the small boy and girl to stand behind Sara. "Walk slowly, children, and remember to go sit beside your parents after your part in the ceremony is done."

"Timothy won't forget." Gladys patted the small boy on the head. "Just like we practiced, darling."

Lester, with Izzie on his arm, stood behind the flower girl and ring bearer.

"This is it, everybody." Gladys came to stand on the other side of the door. "Let's go."

The audience stood as Sara walked down the aisle in steps measured to the music.

Pastor Frank came up the steps that led to the stage and with some difficulty sat in a chair beside the podium. Dr. Henry Faulkner followed him, stood behind the pulpit, and waited until the wedding procession took their places, before he said, "You may be seated."

The music stopped. A hush fell over the audience. Dr. Faulkner spoke in a deep sonorous voice, "Let us bow our heads in prayer.

"Gracious Heavenly Father, bless this marriage, and this young couple as they begin their journey through life together. Help them as they take up their work on the missionary field, to lean on you, and on each other. Help them to remember that a Christ-centered life is the way to keep their marriage ever fresh and new. Help them to know and see that no matter what happens, all things work together for the good of those who love You, those who are called according to Your purpose.

"Bless these families and friends who are gathered here today to celebrate with this young couple the beginning of their life together. I ask this prayer in the name of our blessed savior, the Lord Jesus Christ, Amen"

He lifted his head, introduced Pastor Frank, and then put a low stool behind the podium.

Pastor Frank stepped onto the stool. His head was barely visible over the podium.

"Dear friends, we are gathered together here to..."

Izzie was glowing. Maybe all brides were beautiful. Sara hoped this bride and groom would be happy. They had known each other for such a short time. Her mind wandered back to her own wedding day. She hadn't known Kent then, not really. The truth was she still didn't know him. Until this moment she had been so sure they could work through this problem. What if they couldn't? What if Kent harbored some deep dark secret that would destroy their marriage and their lives? She pushed that notion from her mind and pulled her thoughts back to the present.

Izzie and Andrew lit the unity candle from the two lit candles on either side of the altar. A lump rose in Sara's throat. *Such a beautiful ceremony.*

Dr. Faulkner led the congregation in a closing prayer.

Pastor Frank introduced Izzie and Andrew as Mr. and Mrs. Andrew Faulkner. "Andrew, you may kiss your bride."

Let them be happy, please God. Let them be happy.

The recessional music began.

The bride and groom walked up the aisle and toward the back of the church.

Sara followed. This was a time to rejoice, but her heart was a lump of lead inside her chest.

January 1, 1946
Tuesday Morning

Today was the last day of Mama and Grandma's visit. Tomorrow they would go back to the farm.

Lunch would be a meatless meal, except for the one ham hock she had saved coupons to buy for the black–eyed peas. Grandma would bake a pan of cornbread and Mama would make her famous banana pudding. Mrs. Mac, who was coming to celebrate the New Year with them, would bring a covered dish.

"Good morning, daughter. You are up early." Mama came into the kitchen. "Happy New Year." She poured coffee into a cup and sat down. "Something smells good."

"It's a breakfast casserole. It should be done in about fifteen minutes. I got the recipe from Mrs. Mac." Sara poured a cup of coffee and sat across from her mother. She was glad for some time alone with this woman who was not only her mother, but her good friend.

"I'm hungry," Mama admitted. "Although I don't know how I could be after all the food I put away at the reception last night."

Sara thought about pouring out her troubles to her mother. She reconsidered. Mama and Grandma would be leaving tomorrow. This was a day of new beginnings, a day to celebrate the coming year.

The telephone rang. Sara ran to answer. Who could be calling at this hour of the morning, and on a holiday?

She lifted the receiver, and offered a tentative, "Hello."

"Good morning, Sara, this is Martha."

"What's wrong?" Martha never called her on the telephone. She saw that her 'hired help' did that. Something must have happened to Lester. "Is Lester all right?"

"Lester is fine. He and I have news."

Obviously, it was not bad news, since Martha was not in hysterics. Sara drew a sigh of relief. "That's nice. Tell me about it."

"Not over the telephone. We want to tell you in person. We are coming over for lunch. What time should we arrive?"

"It's—I—"

Martha rattled on. "Lester has never seen your house. It's time he did." She asked again, this time in a more strident tone. "What time should we arrive?"

Sara wanted to say she had yet to issue them an invitation. The still small voice that spoke inside her head stopped her. *Patience my child.* In that moment she knew that if she ever hoped to build a good relationship with her mother-in-law, she must change her attitude.

"Well, are you going to answer?"

"One o'clock. Lunch is at one o'clock. Kent will be pleased you are coming."

"We will be there around twelve. That will give us some time to visit. Goodbye for now." Martha hung up.

"I took your casserole from the oven." Mama stood in the doorway. "I hope that wasn't bad news."

"It was unexpected to say the least. Let me sit down and I'll tell you all about it." Mama sat again. "I'm listening."

"Martha just invited herself and Lester to lunch." Sara sat and leaned back in her chair, shaking her head as she did so. "Mrs. Mac will be here. You know how Martha feels about mingling with those she thinks of as her social inferiors." She couldn't keep the sneer from her voice.

"This is your home," Mama said, "and your guests are just that, your guests. You set the example of how those guests should behave. How they follow your lead is not your problem. For heaven's sake, child, you are not responsible for anybody's actions but your own."

"I'll try to remember that." That acerbic tone lingered in Sara's voice. Mama offered neither help nor sympathy.

"Behave as you think Our Savior would have you to, and remember you are accountable for your actions and your thoughts."

"I will try." For the first time, she understood Mama was offering her sound advice. Why hadn't she seen this before? "Thank you."

"Let's get busy." Mama stood. "Your guests will be here soon."

Chapter Thirty-Nine

January 1, 1946
Tuesday Noon

When Sara told Kent his parents were coming to lunch, he was elated. "I am happy you invited them. I am sure they are pleased."
She couldn't tell him that Martha had invited herself. She did smile and silently vow to change her attitude and, as Mama had said, her thoughts. This was going to be a happy occasion.
Lester rang the doorbell at promptly twelve noon. Had they been parked in the next block, waiting for the exact moment to put in an appearance? *Don't go there.*
They had scarcely come through the door and seated themselves when Mrs. Mac arrived.
Kent once more answered the door. He welcomed Mrs. Mac with a smile and a hearty greeting.
If Martha was disturbed to see her cook arrive as a guest, she didn't show it.
Lester was all smiles. "I hope there's a pie in that dish you are carrying." He stood and took the covered dish from Mrs. Mac. "Let me help you with that load."
Sara immediately began preparations to serve the noon meal. She asked Kent and Lester to move the dining room table into the living room and then added its spare leaves.
Mama and Grandma helped put food on the table. Lunch was ready to serve by twelve-thirty. Sara knew how Martha always insisted that meals be served at a designated time. Mama had said *'Behave as you think Our Savior would have you to, and remember you are accountable for your actions and your thoughts.'* Sara asked everyone to be seated and then requested that Grandma say grace.
"Let's hold hands and bow our heads." Grandma took the hand of those sitting on either side of her. The others followed suit.

Grandma prayed a short, but profound prayer, and raised her head.

Martha stood and tapped the side of her water glass with a spoon. "Lester and I have an announcement to make."

"What are you two up to?" Kent raised one eyebrow. "Come on, out with it."

"We," Martha pointed to Lester and then herself, "are now officially members of the Missionary Bible Church."

"You have been members of the Cathedral Church since I can remember." Kent took a swallow of water. "Are you sure you want to do this?"

Sara choked on her food and grabbed for her water glass.

"We sure are. I like the atmosphere there," Lester said, and then added, "They don't rent their pews neither. It's on a first-come-first–serve basis."

"That's my church," Mrs. Mac reminded them. "I teach a Sunday school class there."

Martha nodded. "I know that, Tessie. I hope you welcome us as the other members have."

Mrs. Mac swallowed, batted her eyes, and replied, "You have my welcome and my blessings."

Grandma clapped her hands and shouted, "Praise the Lord."

"We are positive this is where we belong." Martha sat down.

"What made you come to this decision?" Sara had to ask, even though her better judgment told her she shouldn't.

"As I planned for Izzie's wedding, I was impressed by the church as a whole and each member I met. Gladys Faulkner and I talked about being a Christian. She pointed out so many things to me."

For the first time, mama spoke. "Like what?"

"Like how the Holy Spirit works in believers' lives." Martha answered.

A blush of shame burned in Sara's cheeks. She had never thought to speak to her mother-in-law about anything spiritual. She was as much at fault as Martha was for the animosity that existed between them. *Forgive me, Father.*

Mrs. Mac reached for the salt. The blunt ends of her fingers and the short little finger were smaller replicas of Kent's hands. Sara's mind bounced to the thought that had nagged her for weeks. There had to be some connection.

"Do you think so, Sara?" Kent's question pulled Sara back to the present.

Mama answered the question Sara hadn't heard, coming to her daughter's rescue as she had so many times before. "It's more a tradition than a belief. Eating black-eyed peas on New Year's Day is supposed to bring good luck."

Grandma picked up the conversation. "My mother cooked black-eyed peas on New Year's Day way back when I was a girl. She said there was no need to tempt fate."

""I don't care if they don't bring good luck." Lester crumbled a second wedge of cornbread into his plate and ladled a big helping of black-eyed peas over it. "They sure are tasty."

"Mr. Holden is right." Mrs. Mac touched her napkin to her lips. "These peas are delicious. Who cooked them?"

"Sara did," Grandma said, with a touch of pride. "She comes from a long line of good cooks."

"But nowhere near as good a cook as you are, Mrs. Mac," Sara hastened to add.

Martha's silence disturbed Sara. She sought for a way to draw her into the conversation. Before she could think of something appropriate to say, Lester spoke. "Martha was once a good cook. Remember, son, the delicious pot roasts she used to make?"

"I sure do." Kent smiled. "She was the best cook on the block."

"I am still a good cook," Martha declared, with only a hint of indignation.

"Tell us more about your decision to change churches." Sara changed the subject before Martha could say more.

"It was not without much thought," Martha replied.

"And a lot of prayer, too I would hope," Grandma said. "That's a big step."

"Would anyone care for dessert?" Sara pushed back her chair. "It's banana pudding."

"Bring it on." Lester held a spoon in one fist and a fork in the other.

"Where did you get sugar to make banana pudding?"

"We saved it by using saccharine in our coffee." Mama answered Martha's question as she pushed back her chair, and stood. "I'll help you, Daughter."

Once inside the kitchen Sara grabbed her mother's arm. "Am I imagining things or is Martha being sociable?"

"God moves in mysterious ways." Mama laughed aloud. "Relax, for Pete's sake, and let God work His miracle."

That seemed a good idea. "I'll get the bowls. You get the pudding."

Chapter Forty

January 4, 1946
Friday noon

Sara sat in a back booth of Jack's Café and tried to calm high-tension nerves that made her jumpy as a flea on a hot stove. Would Lester meet her here for lunch?

When she called him Wednesday to make the date, he began to ask questions she didn't care to answer. "What brought this on?"

"I need to talk to you about something I can't talk about in the presence of anyone else." That should silence him.

It only served to pique his curiosity more. "Is this about my son?"

"Will you meet me on Friday at Jack's Café for lunch?" Kent was not his son, not really.

"I'm awful busy on Fridays." He asked again, "Is this something about Kent?"

"I need to talk to you, Lester. It's important. Will you or won't you have lunch with me on Friday?"

"About what, for crying out loud?" He hung on with the tenacity of a bull dog.

"You will find out if you meet me Friday at twelve o'clock at Jack's Café." Sara hung up the telephone and stood waiting for it to ring.

It didn't. She had been so sure Lester would call back. He didn't. Nor did he call the next day.

She wanted to ask Kent if Lester told him of her call but felt she shouldn't.

There was only one thing left to do, show up at Jack's Café at twelve o'clock on Friday

Here she sat, worrying, wondering, and a nervous wreck. She looked at her watch. It was twelve-twenty. She had almost given up hope when Lester walked through the door.

"I am putting my reputation on the line." Lester slid into the seat across from Sara. "Having lunch with a pretty girl in a public place. What if somebody sees me and tells Martha?" The smile on his face said he was joking.

"Thank you for coming." In spite of her jangled nerves, Sara returned his smile. "Lunch is my treat." She took a menu from behind the napkin dispenser and passed it to him.

A pert young waitress appeared with a pad in her hand and her pencil poised. "Are you ready to order now?"

"I'll have the blue plate special." Lester closed the menu. "Bring me some coffee now, put this all on one ticket, and be sure you give it to me."

"No. This is my treat." She didn't want him to be nice to her. That was the one thing she couldn't handle. "I'll have the blue plate special, too."

"I'll put your meals on separate tickets. You can settle the matter between yourselves." The waitress sped away before either Lester or Sara could reply. She returned almost instantly with Lester's coffee, set it before him, and once more beat a hasty retreat.

"This is about Kent, isn't it?" Lester took a quick sip of coffee.

"I want to know how Kent is related to Mrs. Mac." Sara spoke with a boldness she didn't feel. She added in a steady, assured voice, "Don't bother to deny it. I know he is."

Lester's face turned a pasty white. His eyes clouded over with something akin to fear, or was it pain? He took another sip of coffee. After long moments of excruciating silence, he asked, "Whatever gave you such a crazy notion?"

"Is she his mother?"

"Woman, have you lost your mind?"

"If you won't tell me, I will ask Mrs. Mac."

The waitress appeared with their food.

Lester waited until she walked away to say, "If you love Kent, you will let sleeping dogs lie."

"It's because I do love Kent that I do have to know."

"Explain." That one word carried both a command and a promise.

"Kent refuses to even talk about having children. He says he doesn't know anything about his biological background. He says—."

"Did he tell you that?" Lester held up one hand to stop her flow of words.

"He did."

"Here I am, smack dab between the devil and the deep blue sea."

"Is Mrs. Mac Kent's mother?"

"No." Lester loosened his tie. "She is not."

"Then who is? I know you know."

"After all these years, the cat is out of the bag." Lester closed his eyes and grimaced before he opened them again. He pushed back his plate and put both elbows on the table. "Kent's mother was Mrs. Mac's twin sister. She's been dead for a long time."

"Who is his daddy? I know you know that too."

"You're looking at him." Lester put his chin in his cupped hands and stared across the table.

"*You*?" Sara struggled to comprehend what she had just heard. Surprise cramped into her stomach. "You are Kent's Daddy?"

"Before you go jumping to a lot of conclusions, listen to what I have to say." He dropped his arms and ran one hand through his thinning hair. "I never intended for anyone else to know."

This put a different light on everything. "How many people do know?" she asked.

"Mrs. Mac for sure. I got a feeling that Izzie knows." Lester gave his napkin a sling, unfolding it before he laid it across his lap. "Now you know too. Who told you?"

"Nobody told me. I kept noticing the resemblance. You don't have to worry. I won't say a word to Martha." That should ease his mind.

"Martha knows. She has for a long time." Lester looked down at his untouched food, and slid his plate from him. "My appetite just went south. I never meant to have an affair with Missy. It wasn't even an affair. It only lasted a few months. Missy was Kent's Mama's name. Really it was Melissa, but everybody called her Missy."

Sara wanted to tell him to forget the details and get on with his story. The pain in his eyes and the grim look on his face stopped her. She sat waiting patiently, for him to continue.

"I met Missy in 1908. We both worked at The Blue Goose Café. I was the janitor and dishwasher. She was a waitress. I felt sorry for the poor girl. Her sister had moved to another state. She was lonesome, and to tell the truth, so was I.

Martha and me weren't getting along so well along about then. One thing led to another, and before I knew it, I had stepped over the line. I felt awful."

"After a few months, Missy told me it was over. She quit her job and said she was going to another town to live with a cousin." He rubbed his fingers across his forehead. "I tried to forget all about what happened." He stopped and took a deep breath.

"I had no idea." Maybe she *should* have let this sleeping dog lie. Knowing that, Sara still had to ask, "What happened then?"

"About three months later Missy called me. She said she had to talk to me. I didn't think I should see her again, but she insisted. So, I agreed to meet her in the park at six o'clock that evening. That's when she told me she was expecting my baby. I offered to divorce Martha and marry her. She laughed and told me she didn't intend to ever marry any man."

"What did you do?" Sara had always thought of Lester as a shallow, foolish old man. In a heartbeat, her opinion changed.

"I panicked. I was just a kid, barely twenty years old. I said I'd pay her medical expenses and take care of her until the baby came, and then Martha and I would take the baby. I was making big promises that I didn't know if I could keep. Through all my fear and panic, one thought shone perfectly clear. This was a chance to have a child of my own. That was selfish, but that's what I thought."

"How did Martha feel about all this?" Sara looked down at her half-full plate before pushing it from her. Her appetite had followed Lester's.

"I didn't tell her, not that night, anyway. When I got home, Martha was in tears. I was sure someone had told her about Missy and me."

"Had they?"

"No, but that day the doctor had confirmed for sure that she would never have a child. Martha was a basket case. How could I tell her that another woman was having my baby?"

"What did you do?" Sara's heart went out to this aging, sorrowing man.

"I never found a convenient time to tell her. I worked like a dog for the next six months. I sold some of my tools and got a loan from the bank. I made ends meet, but by the skin of my teeth. I had asked the midwife I hired to call me the instant Missy started having birth pains. I wanted to be there when my child was born."

By now Sara was hanging onto his every word. "Did she?"

"No. I got worried. Finally, I got up the nerve to go to Missy's boarding house. When I got there her quarters were empty. She had moved out, bag and baggage. I asked her landlady for a forwarding address. She didn't have one. She told me that two weeks ago, just after her baby was born, Missy moved out. I ask if the baby was a boy or a girl. She said it was a boy."

"Hey, you two. What's going on?"

Sara looked up to see Kent standing by their booth.

Chapter Forty-One

"Later," Lester said from one side of his mouth.

"I'm sorry to disturb your lunch." Kent motioned for Sara to move over and slipped into the seat beside her before addressing Lester. "Mr. Jefferson is in your office. He's kicking up quite a fuss."

"Again? What's he complaining about this time?"

"Something about tires not being rationed anymore." Kent shrugged. "He refuses to talk to anyone but you."

"I don't have anything to do with tires no longer being rationed and why should he care?"

"I asked him that." Kent grinned. "He said he would discuss that with you, and only you."

"I'd better go and see what he's het up about this time." Lester slipped from his seat and straightened his tie. With a wave of his hand, he was on his way.

"Father didn't have time to finish his lunch. I'll take him a sandwich when I go back." Kent turned to face his wife. "Go ahead, finish your meal."

"How did you know where to find Lester?" Sara pulled her plate of cold food toward her. "Have you eaten?"

"I ate the lunch you packed me, but I'll order a sandwich for Father and have a cup of coffee while you finish your meal." He signaled for the waitress.

"I am just now getting acquainted with your father." Sara forked a cold green bean into her mouth and chewed. The bean had the consistency of rubber. "I like him very much."

"I am so glad. He's really an all-right guy once you get to know him." The waitress appeared and Kent placed his order before saying, "I'm pleased you invited him to have lunch with you."

"He told you he was meeting me for lunch?" Sara was surprised by that bit of news.

"Yes, he did. He was quite flattered by your invitation."

"You are so kind to my family and I don't even know your parents, not really."

"So, you thought it was time to get acquainted?"

"In a way, yes." She couldn't tell him she had twisted Lester's arm to get him to be her lunch guest.

The waitress returned and laid two tickets on the table. Sara grabbed for them. Kent was too fast for her. "I'll take care of these."

"This was supposed to be my treat." Sara extended one hand. "Please, I insist."

"No way." Kent stuffed the tickets into his shirt pocket. "I am too happy about seeing my family come together to complain about two meal tickets."

Sara stopped arguing. It was either that or tell the truth about her lunch date with Lester.

"I have to get back to work." Kent drank the last of his coffee and kissed her cheek. "I'll see you later."

For a long time after Kent left her, Sara sat in the booth staring into space and thinking about what Lester had told her. Maybe she should never have raised this issue, but she had. Where did she go from here? One thing she knew for sure. She must hear the rest of Lester's story.

January 6, 1946
Sunday afternoon

Sara wrapped her coat around her as she huddled on the park bench and waited for Lester to show up for their scheduled meeting. She felt like a fool, having to set up a secret rendezvous to talk to her father-in-law. There seemed no other way.

What a can of worms she had opened. "Please, Jesus," she prayed, "let this fiasco have a happy ending." A wan sun had begun its westerly descent. The north wind stirred through the dry branches of the trees. Sara shivered. But not from cold, from anxiety.

Lester appeared far down the pathway. He wore no hat. The wind tossed his thinning hair. He arrived at the bench out of breath and frowning. "Let's get this over fast, 'cause I'd like to get back home before Kent leaves."

"Hello to you, too, Lester." Sara scooted to one end of the bench.

"Hello. Let's get said what has to be said and fast." He sat beside her. "If I re-member right, I left off where Missy had run away, and taken Kent with her."

"That's right."

"I was heartbroken. Somewhere out there was my son, the child I had never seen. The only child I might ever have. I vowed to find him."

"Did you?"

"No." Telltale tears stood in Lester's eyes. One rolled down his cheek. He wiped it away with the back of his hand. "I looked for two long years, but with no luck. Then one day, out of the blue, I got a letter from Missy. I was working when the postman brought it. Martha read it. I had no choice but to tell her everything."

"What did the letter say?"

"Missy told me she was sick, real sick, and didn't have much longer to live. She said I should come get my boy because she could no longer take care of him."

"What did Martha say about all this?'

"I didn't give her a chance to say anything. I told her either she accepted me and my son, or I would take him and we would both leave."

"She agreed to that?" The Martha Sara knew would have never done so.

"Martha wanted a child. She agreed only if she adopted Kent. She would not have him growing up being branded as illegitimate. So, that's what we did."

Sara spoke her greatest fear. "Did she resent him?"

Lester shook his head. "No. Let me tell you why. When we went to fetch him, he was staying with a neighbor. The poor woman had five kids of her own. He was a mess, dirty and his pants were ripped. The other kids were teasing him because he didn't have a daddy. He sat in a corner all by himself. He'd been crying. He wiped his nose on the sleeve of his dirty shirt.

"Martha took one look, and fell in love with him. She told those kids, right off, that I was his father, and that was better than him having a daddy. She also said she was his mother."

"She soon was, legally. The adoption went through without a hitch because I was his real daddy. The day Martha officially was Kent's mother, she cried. That's the only time I ever saw her shed a tear. Now you know. Go ahead and hate me."

"Hate you?" Sara gasped. "How could I? I admire you. Through everything that happened, you took the high road, and did what you thought was right. I love you. How could I not? You are Kent's daddy."

"I'm a sinner," Lester confessed through tears. "I committed the terrible crime of adultery."

"We are all sinners." Sara laid her hand on his arm. "Have you asked God for forgiveness?"

"About a million times."

"Do you know Jesus as your savior?"

"Yes, ma'am. I accepted Him back when I was fourteen-years-old."

Sara's one desire now was to comfort this sad and suffering man. "Jesus paid the price for all our sins when he died on the cross."

"Even adultery?" Questioning hope lit up Lester's face.

"In God's sight sin is sin. He forgave you a long time ago," Sara said, "just like you asked Him to do." She added, "That doesn't mean you didn't pay the consequences of that sin."

"I'm still paying the consequences. I can never tell Kent he is truly my flesh and blood son."

"Yes, you can," Sara argued. "You should."

"Do you really think so?"

"I do. Yes, I do."

"I gotta get out of here before I start bawling in public." He stood and turned to go.

"Can I tell Kent?" Sara called after him.

"And have my son hate me?" Without looking back, Lester continued on his way.

"He won't hate you." Sara pursued him; caught him by the arm and pulled him around to face her. "Don't you see? Now he can know who he is, and we can have the baby I want so badly."

"A baby?" Lester smiled through his tears. "My son's son."

"I can't promise a boy. You might end up with a granddaughter." Sara smiled.

"Go ahead, tell him. I'll take my chances."

"Thank you. Thank you". Sara threw her arms around his neck and kissed his cheek. "Thank you."

She ran all the way home.

Chapter Forty-Two

January 6, 1946
Sunday Evening

Sara sat on the couch, pressing her hands together, and praying as she had never prayed before. She begged God for the right words to say to Kent. She had been so judgmental of Lester and Martha. Would God punish her for that? *I promise, dear, Jesus to be less judgmental if only You*—Words Mama had so often promoted in the past came to her mind. *Be careful how you make bargains with God. He has a way of exacting payment, sometimes in unexpected ways.*
Sara was a child the first time she heard that admonition. In not-too-kind a response, she asked what she should pray for.
"Pray for God's will to be done," and then ask Him for the grace to accept what He knows is best."
Sara fell to her knees and wept tears of repentance. If Jesus could say 'not my will but thine,' as he prayed in the Garden of Gethsemane, how could she dare ask anything more? She stood and walked toward the kitchen with the thought that she would make a good dinner for her husband.
She was staring into the refrigerator when Kent came through the front door.
"Hello. Anybody home?"
"In here."
"Did you miss me?" He came to stand behind her and put his arm around her waist.
"I always miss you when you are gone." Sara closed the refrigerator door. "I was about to start dinner."
"Forget cooking. I will take you out." He kissed her cheek. "Where would you like to go?"
"Some place that's quiet where we can talk." She turned to face him. "I'll get my coat."

They drove to a cafeteria near their house, took their time choosing their food, and then found a booth in the back of the dining room.

"Have you been here before?" Kent asked as he scooted into the seat across from Sara.

"No." Sara shook her head. Telling Kent about Lester was not going to be easy. *Help me, Lord, please*

"Neither have I." Kent stared down at his plate. "The food looks good."

"I have something important to tell you." Sara spread her napkin across her lap. "It will come as a surprise. I hope you will be pleased to hear it."

"I hope so too. The look on your face says I may not be." His brow wrinkled into a frown.

"The other day when I had lunch with Lester." She paused.

"Go on." Kent's frown deepened.

"He told me."

"He told you *what*?"

"Lester is your biological father." Sara blurted out, and then clenched her jaw.

"I don't believe you." Kent's mouth fell open and then closed as his frown converted into a look of surprise. "Is this some kind of joke?"

"It's the truth." Sara lifted one hand. "I swear."

"Did Father tell you this?"

"He did." For better or worse, at least now he knew.

"Maybe you'd better tell me the rest of what Father told you." Kent pushed back his plate, leaned forward, folded his arms on the table and waited.

In disjointed sentences that were often out of sequence Sara told how her suspicion that Kent was related to Mrs. Mac was first aroused. "I confronted Lester and demanded he tell me the truth."

"Father would never keep something like that from me."

"He did," Sara assured him.

"Are you trying to tell me that Mrs. Mac is my mother?"

"She is you mother's twin sister." She was making a terrible mess of this.

Kent slid to the end of his bench and stood. "Let's go."

"Go where?" Sara moved to the edge of her seat.

"To see Mrs. Mac. I am going to get to the bottom of this."

"Wait," Sara called. She stood, picked up her purse and followed him outside, shoving her arms into her jacket as she went.

"Have you been here before?" Kent parallel parked his yellow Oldsmobile in front of Mrs. Mac's residence. It was an old Victorian house that had been converted into four apartments.

"Yes, once. I came here with Izzie." Sara reached for her door handle. "Her apartment is upstairs on the right. The entrance is on the south side of the house."

"Let's get this done." Kent got out of the car and closed the door.

Sara got out and followed him up the walk and around to the side of the house. The outside staircase that led to Mrs. Mac's apartment shook as he started up the steps. Sara grasped the banister and followed him.

Mrs. Mac answered the first rap on her door. "Mr. Kent, what happened to bring you here?"

"May we come in? I need to talk to you."

Sara reached the landing. "We are not bringing bad news." There was no point in frightening the poor woman.

"Sara?" Mrs. Mac questioned. She opened the door wider. "Come in, both of you."

The living room was small, but well-furnished, with an eye for comfort rather than fashion.

"Sit down." Mrs. Mac waved in the direction of a nearby winged back chair.

Sara sat. Kent settled on one end of the settee.

Mrs. Mac sat beside him and clasped her hands in her lap. "You want to talk to me. Why?"

"Sara says you are my aunt. Is that true?"

So much for tact. Sara interrupted, hoping to soften the impact of Kent's blunt words. "Forgive us for intruding this way, but Lester says you are Kent's mother's twin sister. I told Kent and he doesn't believe me."

"Lester told you that?" Mrs. Mac unclasped her hands and laid the right one over her heart. "He broke our pact. How could he do that after all the things he made me promise?"

"Then it's true?" Kent stood and paced across the floor before turning to face Mrs. Mac. "You are my aunt?"

"Yes, I am." Mrs. Mac pointed to the vacant end of the settee. "Sit back down and I'll tell you everything."

Kent came back across the room and sat down. "Please do."

"We had hoped you would never know."

"Who is we?" Kent was on his feet again.

"All the people who love you. Me, Lester, and yes, Martha." Once more she patted the cushion beside her. "Will you please sit down? I can explain."

"I don't think you can." Kent walked to the window, and with his hands behind him, stared outside. "You kept a secret like that from me all those years and you say it's in the name of love?"

Sara sat silent and gnawed her bottom lip. Lester had warned her. Had she listened? No.

"Nevertheless," Mrs. Mac said, "I am going to try."

Sara had started this chaos. She must do her best to make things right again. She pointed to the seat beside Mrs. Mac. "Please listen to what your aunt has to say. You owe her that much."

"Do I?"

She saw in the look he gave her, the intent to refuse. "You most assuredly do."

He shrugged, went back across the floor, and sat beside Mrs. Mac. "I'm listening."

"I didn't know about you until after Missy, your mother, died. I didn't even know she was ill. I lived in another state. We corresponded often, but she never told me about Lester, or you."

"Where was my father when my mother—my birth mother—passed away? Why wasn't he there to take care of her?"

Sara broke into the conversation. "Lester did care for her so long as he knew where she was. They had an agreement. He was going to take you when you were born. Missy must have changed her mind after you got here. When he went to get you, she had disappeared, and taken you with her."

"Wait a minute." Kent waved both hands. "Are you telling me that my mother—my adopted mother—agreed to take my father's child by another woman as her own?"

"She did indeed." Mrs. Mac nodded. "Martha has her faults but never doubt her love for you. In a way I think she is glad that you are Lester's biological child."

"She adopted you," Sara hastened to add.

Tears stood in Kent's eyes. "All these years I have wondered why my real parents gave me away. They didn't. They both loved me."

"Lester still loves you," Mrs. Mac said. "In her own way, so does Martha."

Kent shook his head. "This is a lot to take in at one time."

Sara asked a question she had wanted answered for a long time. "How did you get the job as the Holdens' cook?"

Chapter Forty-Three

January 6, 1946
Sunday Evening

"Later." Mrs. Mac waved Sara's question aside. "First I want to hear Kent's reaction to all this." She turned to her nephew. "Well?"

"I don't know." Kent shook his head as if he was trying to clear his mind. "It will take a while for me to grasp all this."

"You never suspected, not even once?" Mrs. Mac frowned. "Not even when Lester took you as a partner into a business that is worth a small fortune?"

"Why didn't he tell me?" Once more Kent was on his feet. He paced the floor as he rammed one fist into the palm of his other hand.

Sara stood, walked to her husband, and grabbed his wrists. "He wanted to protect you."

"From what?" Kent's jaw tightened.

"From being labeled illegitimate." She tightened her grasp. "You should get down on your knees and thank God that Lester is your father. He could have deserted Missy when he learned she was expecting his child. He didn't. He took care of her." Quick hindsight called to Sara's remembrance how Kent always walked away when she mentioned God or children. She released him and waited for him to retreat.

Kent didn't move. "Why didn't he marry her?"

"He offered." Mrs. Mac stood and came toward them. "Missy told him no. I know this because I read the journal she kept. I found it among her papers after she died." She rubbed the back of her neck with one hand, before saying, "Please sit down, both of you."

Kent retreated to the settee.

Sara moved toward her chair.

Mrs. Mac caught up to her and grabbed her arm. "Not here, sit on the sofa beside your husband."

Sara obeyed, but she moved to the other end of the couch, as far away from Kent as possible.

Mrs. Mac sat in the chair and clasped one hand in the other. "God forgive me. I am about to speak ill of my own flesh and blood. My own *dead* flesh and blood." She paused.

"Yes, go on." Sara moved nearer Kent and took his hand.

"Missy was not a bad person. She was..." After another tense silence, she continued. "Missy liked men. We were sixteen when I caught her with a married neighbor. We had a terrible quarrel. Things were never the same between us after that. Missy left home two years later."

'Where did she go?" Kent and Sara asked in unison.

"I don't know. Just after Missy moved out, I went away to a culinary school, and later got a job as a cook in an up-scale restaurant in Chicago.

"I didn't hear from Missy until Mama and Papa were killed when their car was hit by a locomotive. I came home for their funerals and Missy was there. Our parents' deaths shook both of us. We made up and vowed to never lose touch again. After that, I heard from her regularly for some time. Then she stopped writing. I wrote her several times. The letters always came back with 'moved, left no forwarding address' stamped on them."

"What did you do then?" Sara asked.

"What could I do?" Mrs. Mac shrugged. "I had no idea what had happened or where she was. One day about two years later, I got a letter from her. She said she had been busy and she was sorry she hadn't written sooner."

"Two years?" Kent tightened his hold on Sara's hand. "Did you ask where she had been and what she had been doing?"

"I was too glad to hear from her to start asking questions." Mrs. Mac grasped a chair arm with each hand. "I know now that was a mistake." She dug her fingers into the upholstery.

"This remembering is too much for you." Sara's pity took precedence over her curiosity. "We can talk again later."

"No," Mrs. Mac objected. "Let me say everything there is to tell." She picked up the threads of her story. "After a while Missy stopped writing again. I didn't hear from her for a long time. When she did write, it was to say she was terminally ill. She had a sexually transmitted disease for which there was no cure at that time. She went on to tell me about her little son. She said his father would take care of him and that I wasn't to worry. I took a leave of absence and came back to Houston immediately. Missy died a few hours before I got home. Three days later I buried my sister. Her son was the only living relative I had in the world. I looked through all Missy's papers, hoping to find something that would give me a clue as to where he was."

Sara hung onto Mrs. Mac's every word. "Did you find anything?"

"I found several letters Lester had sent. He sent money each time but he never included a return address. I had a name. I wanted to look, but if I wanted to keep my job, I had to go back to Chicago and show up for work."

"Thank you for telling me." Kent released Sara's hand. "My only regret is I didn't know sooner."

"Don't look back," his aunt told him. "Because you can't change what was."

Sara had yet to learn how Mrs. Mac came to be the Holden's cook. She didn't intend to leave until she had more answers.

"How did you—"

"Become Lester and Martha's cook?" Mrs. Mac completed Sara's sentence. "Yes."

"I will try to make a long story short. I returned to Chicago. In 1920 I met my husband, William. He was a World War One veteran and not in good health. All of my friends said I was crazy to take on such a burden, but I loved him. He was the sweetest, gentlest man I ever knew." She waved one hand. "That's another story. A year later our son Willie was born. Six months after that, William died."

"How sad." Her story was moving, but it didn't tell Sara what she wanted to know.

Mrs. Mac continued. "I dedicated my life to bringing up Willie. He was the joy of my existence. He was killed on Guadalcanal in 1943. When I got the news, I was devastated. I had lost my only child. I was alone in the world. Then I remembered, somewhere I had a nephew. I decided to find him. I quit my job, packed up all my belongings, and moved back to Houston."

Chapter Forty-Four

Kent was visibly moved. "I never knew. I had no idea."

"Go on with your story," Sara urged.

"It wasn't difficult to find Lester. He was a successful entrepreneur with a thriving salvage and used car business. I got a job and after a while, found an apartment. Once I was settled, I went to his business and demanded to see him."

"Did you?" Kent moved restlessly about. "See him, I mean."

"I did. He recognized me immediately and turned pale as a ghost. He demanded to know why I was there. He put on a brave front, but I knew he was scared. I told him not to be. All I wanted was to be a part of my nephew's life."

"What did he say to that?" Kent sat on the edge of his seat.

"He told me that was impossible. He said you were in Europe fighting in the war. I told him that he would make it possible unless he wanted me to tell you the truth the moment you came home. We talked for a long time. We worked out a plan. He would hire me as his cook. When you returned, I could see and be with you. The only stipulation was that I must never tell you that I was your aunt. That was the only way, he told me, unless I wanted you to learn that you were born out of wedlock. I agreed. The only hurtle left was convincing Martha."

"Mother agreed to that?" Kent, eyes widened in surprise.

"Martha has her faults," Mrs. Mac said, "but she would do anything to protect Kent. She not only agreed to me being her cook, she agreed to hire the young woman who worked with me at the restaurant as her maid."

"Was that young woman Izzie?" Sara asked.

Mrs. Mac nodded. "Izzie was the scullery maid at that place. She did all of the dishwashing and much of the sweeping and mopping. The manager treated her like dirt."

Sara's spirits lifted. So many things were falling into place.

January 6, 1946

Sunday Night

It was well past ten o'clock when Sara and Kent arrived home. Sara laid her coat across a chair and put her purse on an end-table. "Would you like some coffee, or do you think it would keep you awake later?"

"I doubt that I will sleep tonight with or without coffee." Kent draped his jacket over Sara's coat.

"I'll make a pot and we can talk." Sara moved toward the kitchen.

Kent followed and sat down at the table. "All of my life I wondered about my biological family and questioned why they gave me away. Now I know the truth. They do love me. They always did. They cared enough to keep their relationship to me a secret."

"Learning the truth is an answer to prayer." Sara measured coffee into the pot and added water. "You know who you are. We can talk about having children."

"I told you in the beginning—" Kent jumped to his feet with a swiftness that startled her. "Excuse me." He turned and was almost to the kitchen door before she realized he was leaving.

She ran after him. He was in the living room when she caught up and grabbed his arm. "Where do you think you are going?"

"Let me go." He tried to shake free.

Sara held onto him. "Not this time, not until you tell me what is troubling you."

"Let it go, Sara." He pried her fingers from his arm and headed for the front entrance.

"If you walk out that door, I won't be here when you get back."

He stopped and without turning said, "If I stay and tell you, then you will go when you know. What difference does it make?"

"I won't leave you, ever. I promise. I love you." His problem ran much deeper than she had ever ventured to imagine.

"Even if you stayed you would hate me." He turned to face her. "I couldn't bear that."

"Can't you see?" Sara extended her hands with her palms up. "This thing that is torturing you is also threatening our marriage. Given time it will destroy you and our love."

"I can't. It's too horrible. Don't ask me to."

Sara sat on the end of the couch and pointed to his easy chair. "If you love me, you will sit down and listen to me." She was gambling and the stakes were high. She was betting that he loved her enough to listen to what must be said.

He stood for what seemed such a long time before he moved to the chair and sat down. "I'm listening."

Sara spoke distinctly and with conviction. Inside she was a shaking mass of fear. "Lester and Martha, and yes, Mrs. Mac too, kept a secret that they should have shared with you long ago. I saw tonight as never before the importance of facing the truth, and the consequences of that truth rather than hiding some secret that grows and festers with the passing of time. Don't do that to yourself. Don't do it to me. Share with me whatever is eating into your soul."

He sat, staring at her with a look of questioning dread in his eyes.

Sara opened her mouth to speak. *Not now, my child.* The voice was inaudible, but it sounded in her head with soft decisiveness. She waited, silently.

Kent stood and walked toward her. Without speaking a word, he sat down beside her and took her hand in his before saying, "It happened in a little village in Italy during the war. I can't remember the name. Don't ask me for a date, because I can't remember that either. All I know is that eight of us were assigned to go before the others and clear out any snipers left in the village."

Sara did some swift calculating. This incident must have happened at least two years ago. All this time her husband had been carrying all this pain around inside him. She touched his cheek with her free hand. "It's going to be all right."

He ignored her gesture, and went on with his story. "The place appeared to be deserted. We fanned out in pairs and began our search. Joe, my buddy, and I were in an old building near the outskirts of the village. So far, we'd seen nothing suspicious. Twilight was turning into night. We relaxed and had a cigarette. That's when a bullet that seemed to be fired from nowhere struck Joe in his arm. "I looked across the narrow street and saw a figure carrying a bundle, dart for an open door and run in in the opposite direction. I yelled 'Halt.' The figure kept running. I shot and he fell to the ground.

"Another bullet whizzed by my head, missing me by inches. In the gathering darkness I barely distinguished a figure on the roof top of the building across the street. I shot and he fell onto the cobblestones below."

Sara saw no reason for Kent to be so upset. "You were only doing your duty."

Kent held onto her hand so tightly that she felt pain. "That's not all of the story. I tore a strip from the bottom of my shirt and bandaged Joe's arm. When I was sure he was all right, I went across the street to see if the men I'd shot were dead or alive. That's when I discovered the first man I shot was not a man, but a woman, a young woman. The bundle she carried was a baby. They were both dead."

Sara closed her eyes and swallowed over the lump in her throat. "You had no way to know." She opened her eyes and searched for more words of comfort. She could find none.

Kent continued. "I kept thinking that the woman had nothing to do with the sniper. Chances were, she didn't know he was there until he fired the bullet that hit Joe. She ran because she was scared. Maybe her only thought was to get her baby and herself out of the line of fire."

Sara failed to see the connection between Kent accidentally shooting a woman and her baby and him not wanting children. "What does that regrettable incident have to do with us not having a family?" She hated asking, but she had to know.

Kent released her hand and stood. "I killed a mother and her baby. I have to live with that knowledge for the rest of my life. Would God's punishment for such a heinous act be to send me a physically deformed or a mentally deficient child?"

She thought of Pastor Frank and his dwarf children. "Whatever God sees fit to send us we will consider him or her a blessing." *Help me, Dear Jesus, to rid him of this terrible fear.*

Kent sat down once more and put his head in his hands. "God has no more use for me. I have committed an unpardonable sin."

"Have you asked God to forgive you?"

He dropped his hands and raised his face to stare at her. "What I did was unforgivable." Tears rolled down his cheeks. "Now you know. And you will hate me."

All this time he had been carrying this terrible guilt around inside him. She moved nearer to him and pressed his head down on her shoulder. "I love you, Kent Holden, and God loves you too. If you knew Jesus, really knew Him, you would know that."

"I found Jesus as my savior when I was fifteen, but drugs and wild living separated me from Him long ago. Now it's too late." He raised his head and moved away from her.

"It's never too late. If you were ever God's child, you still are." A swift and uncontrollable anger swept through her. "The very idea, doubting Jesus' magnificent gift of salvation. We must pray about this."

"I stopped trying to pray a long time ago."

"I am not asking you to try to pray. I am telling you that we, you and I, are going to pray, now." Her anger left as swiftly as it had appeared. "Please, Kent. Pray with me." She reached across the space that separated them, and took his hand. She held onto her husband's hand and poured out her heart to her heavenly father. Her burden lifted and a serene peace filled her soul. She said amen, and waited for Kent to speak. If she had to sit here all night, hanging onto his hand, she would do that.

Chapter Forty-Five

The hushed quiet was becoming unbearable. Still, Sara waited. She recalled Grandma's admonition to "pray it through." Everything was in God's hands now. She whispered, "Not my will but Thine."

Kent spoke in a halting voice. "God, if you are there send me a sign." The words were scarcely out of his mouth when church bells rang in the distance.

"It's a miracle!" Sara exclaimed.

Kent spoke to his Heavenly Father. "Thank You. Now I know you are hearing my most earnest prayer. Forgive me for the terrible crime I committed." He breathed deeply. "Please, dear Jesus."

Sara raised her head. Kent was smiling at her through his tears. "All I had to do was ask." He grabbed Sara in a tight hug. "I'm free. I feel like a new man."

Happiness bubbled up inside her. "I liked the old man."

"The new one is even better." He laughed.

They talked until far into the morning, reminiscing about how they met and deciding there *was* such a thing as love at first sight.

"God brought us together. I know that now." Kent moved nearer and took her in his arms. "Now about that baby He is going to give us…"

"Tell me more." Sara twisted from his embrace and raced toward the bedroom.

Kent laughed and shook his head before turning out the lights and following his wife. "Sara Holden, I adore you."

The End

Other Books by Billie Houston

Asking For a Miracle
Cara's Hero
Discovering Emily
For Jenny's Sake
Honey In the Rock
For Jenny's Sake
John Jacob Worthington Jones
Lucky In Love
Old Maid Bride
Summertime In My Heart
That Scott Woman
The Potter's Wheel
The Road to Jericho
Whither Thou Goest

Poetry:
Brush Country
Four Part Harmony
Chapter And Verse

Cookbook:
Old Butter Will Spoil the Cheese